KEEPERS OF THE NIGHT GARDEN

KEEPERS

OF THE

NIGHT

GARDEN

a novella

LYNN HARROD

Keepers of the Night Garden
Copyright © 2021 Lynn Harrod

This book is a work of fiction. Names, characters, businesses, organizations, places, events and incidents either are the product of the author's imagination or are used fictitiously. Any resemblance to actual persons, living or dead, events, or locales is entirely coincidental.

For information contact www.deerwoodpress.com

Book and Cover design by Lynn Harrod
Edited by Rachel Ann and William McCoy
Photos by Kasper Rasmussen, Alexander Zvir, and Sabrina

ISBN: 978-1-7367234-1-8 (ePub edition)
ISBN: 978-1-7367234-3-2 (Paperback edition)

First Edition: May 2021
Second Edition: January 2022
Third Edition: March 2024

DEER
WOOD
PRESS

For Ana Marie and her love of family.

———————————

1

The print advertising for Lionheart Park Retirement Village boasted of "seaside luxury resort living" offering a "wide variety of daily adventures" for the retiree seeking more during the winter of his life. Nowhere in the brochure was there any mention of cost because such obscene numbers were best left to the consultation, followed by the admission process, which signaled the end of the grand tour. A minute later, the property manager would always smile, lean forward, and offer his pen. "Sign here, please."

The details of the brochure didn't matter, for all twenty-eight rooms of Lionheart Park had occupants for many years and would remain occupied for years to come. New residents arrived and unpacked their bags the mornings after former residents "said their farewells," a somber phrase the staff used. A waiting list with an additional forty-five adventurous retirees hung above the manager's desk, pinned to the bulletin board. Nine names highlighted in yellow denoted families of high interest, seven names in blue highlighted families of high income, and four names in green indicated families who had placed a substantial deposit on a room if one should become available.

The quiet, rural retirement community sat on seven acres of fruit trees and old grape vines along James Way, a cracked four-laner that wound through the Central Coast region of California, just north of the city of Arroyo Grande. Flanked by redwood trees and blessed with a cliffside view of the Pacific Ocean to the rear of the property, "seaside luxury resort living" seemed spot on. To an outsider, Lionheart Park appeared to be worth every penny of the five-figure monthly rate.

Of the twenty-eight residents, twelve lived in the grand, three-story, yellow-and-white Victorian house at the end of the driveway, a narrow gravel road lined with ancient Valley Oak and Gold Medallion trees. The "house folks" received round-the-clock care while the sixteen other residents lived in small studio cottages that dotted the property. They were fortunate not only to each have their own private home, but to still have the independence required. These "cottage folks" could still cook, change their clothes, feed themselves, and use the commode without help. Such mundane acts felt like gifts for the seniors at Lionheart Park.

Eloise Goodwin lived in Cottage #6. Her family didn't request that space when they unceremoniously left her there to live out her remaining years, but she certainly felt blessed for it. Cottage #6 stood at the southern edge of the property next to the "Night Garden," an impressive display of colorful local flora, Greek Revival statuary, and a quarter-mile network of walking paths. From her cottage, the cobblestone and river-rock paths ran north to the other residents and south to a dense redwood forest. Eloise loved that area of the property because she'd long been an avid horticulturist.

The lush garden served as her private paradise, watched over by the beautiful Philomena, a ten-foot granite statue of an angel raising both her wings and one arm to the sky.

Other than Groundskeeper Gunther, who took a weed-whacker to the garden every two weeks, Eloise alone visited the Night Garden. She moved to Lionheart Park on her 78th birthday seven years earlier and assumed that her final home would help her accept old age. Instead, it only made her feel younger as she became the de facto curator of the garden and its earthly treasures. She regarded herself as the ward of the poppies, daisies, verbena, ferns, and pickle weed nestled in cradles of oat grass. She cleaned the dozen smaller statues of playful children and woodland animals. During many a sunrise, she looked up and spoke to Philomena, the towering stone angel always watching over her, greeting her with a simple "good morning" and leaving her with a smiling "goodbye for now."

Eloise sometimes told the angel that she felt grateful for the privacy, grateful for an exquisite garden that seemed entirely hers. As she said the words aloud, she wondered if the angel – or anyone listening – knew that she was actually quite lonely, as were each of the twenty-seven other residents who also kept to themselves within this supposed community.

Eloise Goodwin's desolate days at the home contrasted with the vibrant life that led to it. For thirty-one years, she served legendary barbecue to friendly regulars and visiting tourists at the famous Blue Blossom Inn in Santa Barbara. The next seventeen years were spent enriching children as a Kindergarten Aide at Grover Beach Elementary School. During both careers, she spent her spare time growing California poppies and Ox-Eye daisies, garnering blue ribbons at the annual San Luis Obispo County Fair. Her signature onion pie only ever received white ribbons, though several judges claimed it as their favorite dish, their collective sweet tooth worn thin by the barrage of seasonal preserves, pies, and cookies.

Eloise's long, wild, curly brown hair had succumbed to a single, thick gray braid tied with colorful beads that her students and grandchildren made for her. Though her extended family, blood relatives or otherwise, had moved on to different cities and states, the sparkling beads remained. She wore them as a reminder of how her little ones adored her decades ago. If not for the Christmas cards with the posed studio family photos – everyone smiling and looking to their left – and the birthday phone messages with the rehearsed voices of great-grandchildren she'd never met, Eloise would have completely lost them. Perhaps she had lost them, she often wondered, and those shiny beads and showy flowers were all she had left, a lifetime of caring for friends and family distilled and reduced to the caring of a simple flower garden.

Eloise didn't miss her family, or so she told herself. She didn't yearn for weekly visits or feel scorned by the months between phone calls like many of her fellow residents. Instead, she felt grateful that her kin achieved their own fulfilling lives. She didn't want to burden them with the woes of an old woman who'd enjoyed her time in the world and her ample share of life. She felt content with the simplicity of Lionheart Park and the small circle of friends she made there, even if she rarely socialized with them.

Clayton Cooper lived in Cottage #10, just behind the central house. The tall, lean, self-proclaimed roughneck came across as an unruly curmudgeon to most. A former Lead Engineer for General Motors, Clayton spent his days doting on "Marilyn," his pristine, burgundy-and-white 1959 Cadillac Eldorado Biarritz soft-top convertible. Eloise knew well that the beautiful automobile was a rare collectors' item for Clayton reminded everyone daily as he cleaned her red leather interior and polished her chrome bumpers in the old horse stables to the side of the central house. For many at the home, watching Clayton pamper his Eldorado while regaling them with anecdotes was better than TV.

Like Clayton and the other residents, Marilyn had long retired, her days now spent parked and shining in the morning sun. There would be no more road trips for her, no more Cooper children to shuttle to Pismo Beach or farther north to Half Moon Bay. She would never again cruise along The Embarcadero in San Francisco or wander down Highway 99 through the Central Valley during the breathtaking Blossom Trail season. At Lionheart Park, Clayton remained as her only passenger, occasionally taking her around the property, a five-minute drive every few months.

Helene Vasquez lived beside Eloise in Cottage #7. A retired high school Biology teacher, the fit and alert woman followed a pseudo-vegetarian diet and self-guided chair yoga routine. She kept busy by reading, sewing, and serving as a prominent board member of the Morro Coast Audubon Society, a group of professional and amateur ornithologists that monitored the many birds of the Central Coast.

In recent years, Helene became obsessed with online news of the atrocities of the world and fell victim to gripping agoraphobia. Her participation in the Audubon Society continued within her four walls via biweekly phone calls and monthly video conferences. She limited her birdwatching to the robins, swallows, and doves she spied from the deck of her cottage. Though Helene's door always remained shut, Eloise occasionally visited her. She'd bring a homemade blueberry coffee cake or tray of cinnamon rolls, hoping to coax her out onto her deck, so long as Helene provided the fresh-ground coffee with plenty of Splenda and cream.

Virginia Ortega lived behind Eloise in Cottage #5. A chubby little woman with a constant smile, Virginia was a former jeweler, baker, and small business owner from Half Moon Bay. She often met Eloise in the Night Garden at dawn, her advanced arthritis be damned. The burning pain in her joints was worth the short trek to the garden where the two ladies would sit on Eloise's favorite bench facing the redwoods. Together, they watched the sun rise through the redwoods, fed the visiting birds, and talked about their families' past and present lives. Despite rarely getting a visit or phone call, they agreed they did a fine job of raising such upstanding youth and felt grateful to have had the chance.

Eloise's circle of on-off friends included more than fellow residents. She considered her caretakers friends as well.

Property Manager Vicki Carl had an office on the first floor of the central house. Her early goal in life was to become a dancer in Broadway productions. A knee injury sidelined her ambition, landing her in the thankless job of running Lionheart Park, though she tried not to express her regrets and frustrations with her residents. Her all-business, monotone voice not fooling anyone, Vicki's affection for her "twenty-eight grandparents" was clear.

Dr. Thomas Flowers served as the park's physician. For a time, he arrived weekly to tend to his elderly patients at the home, only to visit more frequently over the years, to where a room on the second floor of the house remained reserved for him. Rumors spoke of a crumbling marriage that brought him to Lionheart Park more often, but Eloise refused to dwell on such cruel speculation. She admired Dr. Flowers and valued the time he spent with each resident, never hurrying them or making them feel like afterthoughts. From what she observed, the residents were his foremost priority.

Rounding out her circle of "friends" was Nurse Koob-Hnoov Soung, known simply as "Nurse Kim" to the staff and residents. Nurse Kim lived on the third floor of the central house, always on-call. With a background in Senior Care, Kim never once gave the impression that her job was a stepping stone to a greater career or something she settled for in lieu of failed dreams. She loved her job and genuinely cared for the elderly at the home, and Eloise valued their relationship.

Stemming from her love of literature and theater, Eloise had always considered her life an unfolding story, and she kept that idealistic view in her old age. The home served as its backdrop, her friends as the supporting characters.

They would all be witness to the miracle to come in the thick of the night, in the redwoods beyond the garden.

2

Eloise sat alone in the Night Garden on Sunday mornings. On those days, Virginia remained in her cottage, praying the rosary, asking The Lord for good health. She extended the holy request to both her distant family and nearby neighbors. Eloise always brought two cups of coffee to the garden for Virginia sometimes forgot what day it was and joined her on the bench.

Caw-caww!

One particular Sunday morning changed Eloise's life.

Crok-kraa-kik-cawww!

If only Virginia or Groundskeeper Gunther were there to share the moment.

Croak-kraa-kraa-kra-cawww!

Sitting in her favorite spot – a eucalyptus Adirondack bench in front of Philomena – she stared out at the tall redwoods beyond the garden and heard a strange distress call. From within the forest came a mixture of hoarse caws, rattles, and clicks, rising and falling in the morning mist.

Croak-klik-kraa-klik-cawww!

Defying Nurse Kim's order to never venture past the three-foot-tall rock wall of the garden, Eloise left her cups of coffee on the bench and ventured into the trees.

Following the strange, sharp sounds, she discovered a glade guarded by seven immense redwoods, where a crow flailed on the ground, partially covered by ferns. Several other crows stood gathered around, and Eloise couldn't determine if they were assaulting the poor bird, mourning his fading life, or crying out for help. Her heart decided it was the latter. She knelt to examine the helpless creature.

The small black bird – the size of a newborn kitten – laid on its side, one of its wings painfully bent, with several bloody slashes across its face. Someone or something had attacked it. She wondered again if it was the grim flock that surrounded her.

Staring into the still marble eyes of the bird, Eloise's fear and hesitation surrendered to mercy. She picked up the crow and cradled it in her arms like a baby, wrapping it in her macramé scarf. Knowing that she was breaking the rules, she looked around anxiously as if Nurse Kim or Manager Vicki would suddenly step out from behind a tree and scold her for interacting with the surrounding wildlife.

Eloise carried the bird through the woods, past the rock wall, past the flowers and statues of the garden, returning to her cottage. She was careful not to be seen or heard. With no witnesses at such an early hour, she felt sure she could care for the creature in secret and release it back into the forest that same day.

Had she known that the rehabilitation of a wounded crow would consume her life and earn her the disdain of the other residents, she might have left the defenseless animal in the glade for the wild to claim.

Had she known how this little bird would forever change the lives at Lionheart Park, she would surely have swaddled it in her scarf without a moment of hesitation.

The crow stood on Eloise's cluttered desk. No longer flailing about, it simply stared at her, not once disturbing the small potted succulents and perennial seedlings beside it.

"Such a gentleman," Eloise remarked in her soft, soothing voice, amused that she was talking to a crow in her cottage. "I was afraid that your caws and cries would draw attention, but here you are, perfectly quiet and so well behaved in a stranger's home. I wish more people had such etiquette."

Eloise gathered supplies she assumed she'd need – a roll of gauze, a bottle of rubbing alcohol, a Pyrex cup of warm water, and some popsicle sticks she'd been saving for a diorama, in case the little bird needed a splint. Looking at her supplies laid out across her bed, she admitted to herself that she had no idea what to do, and that all these human medical conventions might be pointless with a wounded crow.

She picked up the telephone on her desk, bypassing the cell phone issued to her by Manager Vicki. The modern gizmo proved too complicated for her and ultimately unnecessary with her trusty old Princess Slimline plugged into the wall.

Scrutinizing a list of names and numbers on her mini-refrigerator, she held the phone receiver in her hand, unsure exactly who to call for help. She couldn't call her fellow residents for rumors spread like wildfire at Lionheart Park. Nothing was more ripe and juicy than someone breaking the rules. She couldn't call any of the staff, for they'd only take the bird away from her, likely abandoning him in the trees.

Eloise felt bad for assuming the worst in them. She took a moment to consider what each member of the staff might actually do.

Manager Vicki would simply tell someone to deal with the bird. She had her hands full with twenty-eight residents' problems. Though she had nothing against animals, the little bird surely wouldn't make her personal to-do list.

Nurse Kim knew nothing about animals, something she'd been ashamed to admit on more than one occasion. Years ago, Helene took in a stray cat. Nurse Kim brought it leftover dinner scraps of meatloaf and fried onions as if it were a pig or a dog. If she knew about the crow, she'd simply defer to Vicki.

Dr. Flowers might help the crow, if only to calm Eloise's heartache. There'd been many times he went out of his way to quell a resident's anguish, petty as it may have been. Four years prior, Clayton forgot to park and cover Marilyn in the horse stable, and a storm broke off her antenna as she sat in the driveway. The proud old goat couldn't speak for fear of crying in front of everyone. Dr. Flowers took it upon himself to drive a rainy hour south to Lompoc for a custom replacement. A wounded crow that was dear to Eloise's heart would have indeed been a priority for him, but he unfortunately had business away from the home that day.

Custodian Eli Hyde, full of machismo, prided himself on being a no-nonsense man, which meant anything that didn't personally interest him was nonsense. Fancying himself a rugged individualist and a man of nature, he'd likely stomp on the crow to put it out of its misery and toss it in the Dumpster. He'd liken the murder to an act of mercy.

The home's resident physical therapist, Billy "Skinny" Fykes, treated the residents well enough, but often displayed questionable morals. The young man once spent weeks encouraging the residents to live a "minimal life" by discarding the clutter in their homes. He told them that anything they didn't use daily took up valuable space in their lives and in their minds, causing them undue stress, and he offered to take it all off their hands free of charge. Rumor had it that the magnanimous Skinny Billy pawned everyone's "clutter" – vintage clothing, antique record players, music boxes, jewelry cases, old books and magazines – for a tidy profit, for that seemed to be in the foreground of everything he saw. Since there was no money to be made from a wounded crow, the bird would be a nuisance to him. He'd smile and assure Eloise that everything would be okay, only to dump the crow behind the three-foot rock wall of the garden.

Groundskeeper Gunther Groom had a kind heart, but feared repercussions from his superiors. He had a wife and four children to care for, children who attended "magnet" schools of higher learning that required his generous donations of time and funding. Understandably, his job held more importance than any one resident's secret dilemma. Surely, little Bernardo's plight paled beside Gunther's family's needs.

"Bernardo," Eloise said to the bird as the name came to her. "That's what I'll call you, little one. It's much better than just calling you 'bird' or 'crow,' don't you think?"

Bernardo The Crow simply stared at her from his spot on the desk, like a good little boy who placed his complete trust in the old woman.

Eloise ran her fingers down the list of names, stopping at "Edie," the first person who she felt might help without incident, without a tit-for-tat, if only she was available.

"I have to call Edie," she said to Bernardo with dread. "The last time I spoke to her was at Randall's funeral. The poor girl has her own problems, and I hate to burden her, but I don't think I have a choice, do you?" Bernardo continued to stare at her, standing between potted aloe vera. "You're right," she said to the silent bird. "She's bright, nearby, and the most qualified to help us. I'm being foolish, afraid to call my Little Butterfly. She may have forgotten me, but the girl is still family."

Eloise dialed the phone.

3

Edie Goodwin was Eloise's oldest granddaughter, a "girl" who had just turned forty. She spent three years studying veterinary medicine while working at the Santa Barbara Museum of Natural History, only to abandon her studies when she became engaged to her supervisor, Randall Welsh, a Botanist who succumbed to a long battle with cancer a month shy of their wedding date. Realizing their limited time, they soon planned on being wed in his hospital room, within the last four walls he'd likely ever see. Sadly, Randall lacked the strength to even make it to the altar at the foot of his bed. On the Friday evening before their Sunday nuptials were scheduled, while Edie was at home hemming her wedding dress, Randall died peacefully in his sleep. At least there would be no more pain for him, his worries in this world ended.

Nurse Kim took Eloise to the funeral service.

That was six years ago.

To cope with the loss, or perhaps just to distract her from it, Edie threw herself into her work. She assumed the job of her late fiancee, making the museum her new career, her way of keeping his spirit alive. With no husband or children, she applied her maternal love toward caring for the exhibits and assumed that the rest of her life would be among the museum's faculty and plants and dinosaur bones.

Edie felt unsure and concerned when "Lionheart Park" appeared on the screen of her ringing cell phone.

"Edie Goodwin," she said, answering her phone.

"Little Butterfly, how are you?" Eloise said on the other line. "How are things at the museum?"

Startled to hear her grandmother's voice after so many years, Edie ignored the pleasantries and cut the point. "Gramma? What's wrong? Are you alright?"

"Me? Oh, I'm fine. They treat me well here."

"So, what's the problem?"

"What problem? Can't I call my Little Butterfly to see how she is?" As she spoke, Eloise realized that her Little Butterfly hadn't been little in decades, and the distance between them felt much farther than the eighty miles between Santa Barbara and Arroyo Grande.

"I'm fine, too, I suppose," Edie said, confused, still waiting for grim news. She'd come to expect it from family calls.

"I admit, there is another reason I'm reaching out. I have a wounded bird here in front of me. A crow. I don't want to make him worse with my flurry of bandages and ointments. I need your advice."

"Gramma, I'm not a doctor. If you want to save your crow, you need to bring him to a vet."

"They'll take him from me," Eloise said, pleading. "I just want to patch him up and send him on his way before anyone is the wiser. Will you help, please?"

Edie couldn't deny that she felt little attachment to her family. They'd never been the emotional type. It simply wasn't in their DNA. When her parents, siblings, and cousins moved away from California, scattering to Oregon, Florida, Illinois, and Vermont, it felt like an escape. Indeed, it served as a mass exodus to all involved.

The Goodwins had no farewell parties, only trucks carting away boxes and furniture in the middle of the night. During Christmas and Easter and the many birthdays in between, no luggage was packed or plane trips booked. No phone calls were made lasting longer than five minutes, no family gatherings took place at their old home in Grover Beach. Perhaps it came from Edie's stern father's disregard for sentiment. Perhaps it rose from their early years of poverty and the good-riddance feeling of fleeing their Central Coast blue-collar life of struggle.

Thousands of miles away, the family patriarch Oscar Goodwin – Edie's father, Eloise's son – eventually achieved the upper-class status he longed for, affording him the ability to keep his widow mother safe and cared for on the outskirts of Rancho Grande Park, minutes away from where they all once lived and loved together. It served as an ideal solution for a man who loved his family enough that he wished them well, but not enough to actually take part in their daily lives.

Edie processed her regrets, notions of what could have been, what should have been, while speaking to her grandmother about something as insignificant as an injured crow.

"What's wrong with it?" Edie said, relenting.

"Something attacked him," Eloise said. "He has slashes across his face, and one of his wings may be broken."

Lynn Harrod

"Is he in shock?"

"How would I know that?"

"Does he look weak? Does he respond to you? Can you see him breathing normally?"

"I don't think Bernardo's in shock, Butterfly," Eloise said.

"Bernardo?"

"He's standing in front of me, on my desk, listening to our phone call. You're on speakerphone, you should know."

Edie laughed at the idea of a crow eavesdropping on them. She'd forgotten how whimsical her Gramma could be. "Look at his eyes," Edie said. "Are they both open? Both black? Same size?"

Eloise took a moment to examine the bird's eyes. "Yep."

"Is he nodding his head? Is he breathing okay? Dangle a tissue in front of his beak. It should move with a rhythm."

"Yep and yep," Eloise said, hopeful. She knew she made the right call.

"And you say he's standing?"

"He's standing right here. In fact, I'm keeping my hand in front of him. I don't want him walking onto the phone and hanging up the call."

"Alright," Edie said with a sigh, accepting the task. "I think we can do this, Gramma. I'm gonna talk you through it."

Bernardo's stay at Eloise's cottage extended well past a day. With his left wing wrapped in torn gauze, the crow walked and hopped around the studio cottage, following his host wherever she went. Her first instinct was to return to the forest and dig up worms for him. On her granddaughter's advice, Eloise instead fed Bernardo small-pellet kitten food, hard-boiled eggs, and lots of nuts and seeds.

She started leaving her cottage an hour earlier each day so Bernardo could roam the Night Garden before sunrise. She did this every morning, hoping that one day his wing would be healed enough that he'd fly away and rejoin his brothers and sisters. After a week, she stopped hoping for a quick recovery. She enjoyed having a roommate, a little bird courteous enough to keep his cawing sounds soft as he toddled alongside her, hopping onto the rock wall that encircled the garden.

It wasn't long before Virginia learned of Eloise's secret friend. The two old ladies sat at their bench in the garden as usual, drinking coffee, breaking apart a stale French baguette for the visiting swifts and swallows and robins, now joined by a crippled crow. Though small for a crow, he was three times the size of the other birds, his black feathers contrasting with their bright, colorful plumage and the array of flowers around them.

"Bernardo?" Virginia said. "How wonderful. What inspired that name?"

"I could tell you it came from 'Zorro,' my favorite series of adventure novels," Eloise said. "I could tell you it was the name of the hero's mute assistant, which is true." Eloise watched the crow interact with the tiny birds. "But I'd be lying, Virginia. 'Bernardo' was my husband's name."

"Bernie Goodwin was actually Bernardo?" Virginia said, gasping at the revelation. "Who else knew that he..."

"Nobody knew. Nobody needed to know. Not back then. Folks accepted us as a couple."

"My goodness, Eloise," Virginia said, dropping the outdated controversy. "I take it you were Bernie's Zorro?"

"He certainly thought so," Eloise said. "But he was the real hero of our adventure, and he's the one who fell in battle." She'd always told herself that the war presented itself as her husband's time of glory, and that his death played a role in the freedom they enjoyed each day, a consolation that faded over the years.

Virginia silenced herself, not wanting to rip open old wounds. She tore off the end of a baguette and handed it to Bernardo at her feet. "His wing seems better," she said. "But he's still here."

"He'll fly off soon," Eloise said. "Everyone leaves eventually."

"Yes," Virginia said. "He'll leave you. But he just might visit you, if there's bread and eggs to be had."

"There always will be."

4

Ten days into Bernardo's recovery, the morning gathering of birds grew as other crows landed in the Night Garden. Virginia ensured that plenty of fresh bread sat in her hand-painted tote bag when she made the morning trek to the garden bench an hour earlier to join her friend. At first, she felt uneasy sitting with her in the dark, but the growing murder of crows actually made her feel safe.

"Murder?" Eloise asked.

"That's what they call a flock of crows," Virginia said. "Helene told me. Such a morbid name for such a fine group of gentlemen."

"You told Helene?" Eloise said, realizing that Virginia always had a hard time keeping secrets. The rumor mill served as her primary entertainment.

"Only her," Virginia said. "She loves birds, she won't spill our secret. I promise."

"Regardless, let's keep an eye open for staff, especially Eli or Billy. I don't rightly trust them." Eloise's friend nodded in agreement.

Unlike Nurse Kim and Dr. Flowers, who'd displayed genuine affection for the residents, Custodian Eli Hyde and Physical Therapist Billy Fykes clearly worked there for a paycheck and nothing more. While there was nothing wrong with working solely for money, that attitude did nothing to endear them to the seniors who called Lionheart their home.

"Bernardo is almost ready to fly," Eloise said. "I can feel it. It'd be a shame if they took him away while he's still weak and helpless."

"We won't let that happen, dear."

The two elderly ladies became three as Helene found the courage to leave her cottage for the first time in years. The sight of Bernardo standing on Eloise's lap proved too much for an old "birder" like her to witness from afar, through the lenses of her antique binoculars.

When Eloise saw Helene at the break of dawn, wandering down the path to the Night Garden, she had mixed feelings. She felt paranoid that her secret had slowly leaked, but also proud that Bernardo inspired Helene to put down her binoculars and venture from her deck to the garden below. Bird-watching is more fulfilling up close.

The colorful little sparrows and robins were always cute, with their comforting little chirps and bright, puffed chests, but the murder of crows – each bird bigger than the last – offered a fierce, fascinating, intimidating display.

"It's funny," Helene said. "I've seen them everywhere, all my life, but I'd never thought much of them."

Helene had long regarded crows as common scavengers, not worth her attention as she focused solely on rare or ornate bird species. She likened it to a collector of exotic insects being drawn to a colony of worker ants or a professional show dog breeder becoming entranced by a common street mutt. But sitting with her friends on the eucalyptus Adirondack bench in the twilight of the Night Garden, with twenty crows gathered at their feet as Virginia fed them stale sourdough, made Helene rethink her passion for birds. If only her peers at the Morro Coast Audubon Society could see her interact with them so freely, petting them, feeding them seeds and bits of overripe banana. If only she could share the details of her mornings with them during their weekly video conferences. She'd be the envy of the council.

"He's an American Crow," Helene said, thumbing through a guidebook, as she gazed at Bernardo standing on Eloise's lap. "About fifteen inches long. That's considered medium size among Corvus."

"He's my red-blooded American boy," Eloise said.

"Corvus?" Virginia asked.

"That's a crow's genus," Helene said, "within the family Corvidae."

"Yes, of course," Virginia said, not appreciating her friend's know-it-all "birder" tone.

Helene referenced her guidebook and jotted notes on a memo pad, sketching the black birds and documenting their every move. "It's unusual to see so many different crows together in one flock. Very rare."

"Why is that?" Eloise asked.

"Normally, a flock comprises just one, maybe two species. This group is a spectrum of the genus. I can't explain it."

"It's a 'murder' of crows, dear, not a flock," Virginia said, proud to correct her well-meaning but over-educated friend for once. "You told me that."

"Technically, yes, it's a murder," Helene said. "But that's such an antiquated, absurd term that rose from superstition. It paints them in a harsh light. Birders only use that term when writing a thesis. In the field, we just call them 'flocks.'"

"I quite like 'murder,' myself," Virginia said. "They're the 'bad boys' of the bird world, like a gang in black leather jackets, even though they're sweethearts."

"True, they normally are," Helene said. "I can't explain that either." She took photos of the crows with her trusty old Nikon 35mm camera, assigning names to several of them as she continued her notes.

"Butch" was another medium-sized crow, slightly larger than Bernardo, a 21-inch Rook that normally ate mostly carrion, though he seemed content with their sunflower seeds and peanuts.

"He's a Rook," Helene said, puzzled. "I think I see a few more. But how can that be?"

"Why is that a big deal?" Virginia asked.

"There are no Rooks in North America," Helene said, checking her guidebook. "They live in Asia, Europe, and parts of Great Britain. How can they be here?"

"Brandywine" was the smallest of the bunch at twelve inches, a black-and-brown House Crow that let out soft chirps to greet them. Because of her diminutive size, Helene surmised she was one of the few females in the flock.

"Boxer" was easily the largest crow, a 27-inch Raven that feasted on carrion. The massive predator's loud caws threatened their peaceful sunrises. One would normally avoid close contact with such an aggressive, unpredictable bird, but he seemed at peace with the women in the garden.

The ladies shared their enrapture with the murder every morning, even as their numbers swelled to three dozen. Their swallows and robins and finches – often prey for birds like Boxer – soon kept their distance until the day only a sea of black awaited them in front of the bench. The sight of so many crows among the flowers and atop the statues was the stuff of nightmares, but Bernardo's bond with Eloise, and the tote bags full of bread and seeds and eggs, kept their mornings civil.

Helene's newfound appreciation for them pushed her to learn more, dusting off long forgotten books about Corvus from her closet.

"Learned anything new about our gang?" Virginia asked one morning.

"Crows are among the smartest animals on Earth," Helene said. "Their vocabulary is close to three-hundred distinct caws and calls. They exhibit complex problem-solving intelligence and can long remember people's faces, even after only one glance."

"So, you're saying they know us?" Eloise asked.

"Oh yes, they certainly do," Helene said. "In their own way, they've given us names as well. They know the difference between you and me and other residents."

"I'm glad we're on their good side," Virginia said, keeping an eye on the bustling crowd at her feet.

"They're still wild animals, Virginia. Predators. Don't get so comfortable so quickly."

"They won't hurt us," Eloise said. "Bernardo won't let them."

Eloise awoke one morning to find Bernardo standing at the door, waiting for the daily pilgrimage to the Night Garden. After feeding him a bowl of eggs and rolled oats, she threw her macramé scarf around her shoulders and opened the door for him. Instead of trotting out in front of her like a steadfast guard, he remained at the doormat, as if trying to grab her attention.

Spread out on the rattan doormat was a collection of assorted items – bottle caps, shiny ocean rocks, arrowheads, broken light bulbs, and pieces of colored glass worn smooth by the shore.

"Who brought us these little delights?" she asked the bird with a grin. "An admirer of yours? Perhaps an admirer of mine?"

The following morning, Eloise discovered more "gifts" from her winged friends – buttons, nuts and bolts, paper clips, Lego blocks likely snatched from children vacationing on the beach. The most valuable item was a golden earring with an embedded pearl, glittering in the moonlight.

Eloise treasured her little gifts and the company the murder provided. It gave her a warm feeling she hadn't thought she'd ever experience again. These birds looked forward to seeing her at sunrise, showing their appreciation with shiny trinkets that one would normally expect from a small child. With her human family far and away, her bird family eagerly awaited her each sunrise in the garden, sitting atop the rock walls and Greek stone statues, cawing with excitement as she approached with Virginia and Helene and their coffees not far behind.

The collection of daily gifts soon became a pile on Eloise's desk. She didn't have the heart to discard them, but couldn't think of what to do with them other than store them in Tupperware containers in her closet. She spotted a diorama in the corner of the room that ten-year-old Edie made for her thirty years prior, depicting a farmhouse in autumn, complete with a candy-corn pumpkin patch and tiny lollipop scarecrow. The girl and her grandmother crafted it together for a fifth-grade class project.

Eloise always treasured the memory, but was now seeing the value of the diorama itself.

Using the pile of tiny gifts, Eloise created a shoebox diorama that told the story of how she met Bernardo The Crow. A three-inch piece of black ribbon with a button eye laid within a forest glade of fern leaves over green felt as a woman made of drinking straws and a coffee filter dress knelt down beside it. Behind her was a bench crafted from pencils and popsicle sticks. The surrounding trees comprised stacked beads, pebbles, and shells. Clouds of white cotton balls rolled across a painted night sky with ocean rocks and bottle caps for stars while the earring's pearl shined down as the moon.

During the construction of the detailed scene, Bernardo watched closely, turning his head only to look at his host. Twice he picked up a rock and plopped it into the shoebox, prompting Eloise to incorporate it somehow. Was he giving her random items from the pile out of affection? Was he knowingly contributing to the little scene? Either way, Eloise considered his additions the most important elements of the diorama.

"There you are, little man," she said to her bird. "That's the day we met. That's the day I adopted you." Hearing her words a moment later, she thought of the eventual day Bernardo would fly off into the sky and leave her at Lionheart Park, as so many others did. She told herself that she wouldn't blame him for choosing the vast sky over the confines of her studio cottage and the walled Night Garden, but she couldn't promise there would be no tears.

5

Virginia didn't come to the garden one Saturday. Her son Paul had promised to visit that day, so she spent the morning preparing her cottage for him. He had important business an hour north in Paso Robles and wanted to drop by with his young daughter, Polly. As much as Virginia wanted to see her son, she especially looked forward to seeing her granddaughter. She'd had only seen Polly twice since moving to the home, as Paul rarely traveled to California.

A bright, young child would have breathed new life into Lionheart Park, and Virginia had the day planned. She imagined spoiling Polly with fresh jam cookies, laughing over old photos of her father in his high school theater days, and giving her a tour of the village. She'd show off her granddaughter to the other residents with pride, pointing out her excellent grades, her artwork, and her musical talent with the trombone and euphonium.

Forty minutes after noon – when Paul was supposed to have arrived – he called to tell Virginia that his important business meeting had been moved to a video conference. He cancelled his flight and stayed home in Arizona, apologizing to his mother for the late notice. Virginia said she understood but neglected to tell him she'd been standing at the head of the driveway awaiting him, a plate of jam cookies in hand, eyes wide with excitement each time she spied any type of "family car" approaching on James Way.

Paul promised that he'd return to California and visit "in a few months," a vague measure of time that meant he had no plans to see her anytime soon.

As she'd always done, Virginia hid her disappointment and heartbreak. She told him how proud she felt about having such a smart entrepreneur for a son, promised to send him cookies, and hung up the phone wishing him well in his business conference. Paul hung up first.

"I had my time, and now he's living his," Virginia told herself, sad to find no comfort in her son's budding career.

Clayton Cooper stood nearby, having just finished waxing the hood of his beloved Marilyn in front of his fellow residents. He'd boasted about the classic Cadillac for nearly two hours, regaling everyone with stories of his service in the Marines and his civilian life in San Luis Obispo as a family man, council member, and award-winning car salesman. Seeing Virginia alone on the driveway, he put aside his tales when he recognized the despair on her face as she finally hung up her end of the phone call. He put down his buffing pads and approached her, wiping wax off his hands onto his denim overalls.

"Paul ain't coming, is he?" Clayton asked, his gruff voice masking his concern.

"The boy has business to take care of," Virginia said.

"He ain't no boy no more though, is he?"

"Not for a long time now." She handed him the plate of jam cookies. "Share these with your audience."

Clayton took the cookies, realizing who they were meant for. "Nah, forget them, they got plenty of sweets. Kim brought them Krispy Kreme."

"She's always so thoughtful."

"But don't you worry none, I'll eat 'em. Hey, how about we sit in the Caddie? I ain't planning on taking her for a cruise, but Rock Oldies AM is playing a Freddy Fender marathon. I know you have a soft spot for the guy."

"Maybe later," Virginia said with a smile. "I need to walk around and clear my head."

Clayton knew her pain. He'd been in her shoes countless times, standing alone at the start of that long gravel driveway, as had many of the residents. "Good luck," he said. "My head ain't been clear for years. Only time I feel alright is when I'm with Marilyn."

In no hurry to return to her tidied-up cottage, which would only remind her of the sunny day with her son and granddaughter that almost was, Virginia wandered about the property and ended up at Eloise's open door.

"Virginia?" Eloise said. "I thought you'd be with Paul and Polly."

"He had to cancel," Virginia said. "They're coming to visit another weekend."

Eloise knew what that meant. "You wanna talk about it, Love?"

"Another time," Virginia said. She spotted a curious box on Eloise's desk. "Right now, I'd like to see what that is."

"Yes! Come look at what Bernardo and I made!"

Stepping through the doorway, Virginia didn't expect to see Eloise's cottage in such disarray, with piles of "gifts" in all corners of the room. It was an overwhelming sight, as was the box, an obsessively crafted diorama.

"When did you make this?" Virginia asked.

"Two weeks ago, but I didn't dare bring it to the garden. I wasn't sure how the crows would react to seeing their precious tributes glued inside a shoebox."

"Such a marvelous little scene," Virginia said. "You're quite the artist."

"It wasn't all me," Eloise said. "Bernardo helped create it."

After examining the intricate detail of the diorama, Virginia eyed the overwhelming piles of gifts surrounding them. Eloise noticed.

"They keep bringing me things," Eloise said. "I'm not sure what to do with them all."

"Heavens, don't throw them out."

"Surely not."

Virginia picked up a handful of shiny ocean pebbles and scraps of metal. "You could make jewelry out of them."

"That sounds nice, but I wouldn't know where to begin."

"I do."

Unlike Clayton, Virginia never bragged about her former life. She'd spent thirty years as a jeweler for a small company in Half Moon Bay, crafting costume necklaces, bracelets, and rings for tourists. She especially loved watching children wearing her novelty rings. Early in her retirement years, she continued to create jewelry to sell at the Berryessa Flea Market in San Jose. With six-thousand vendors across 120 acres it was – and remains – the largest flea market not only in California but the world. The two-dozen vendors around her booth became her second family for many years. They, too, had become a distant memory.

"Maybe you can help me?" Eloise asked. "I don't know if my sausage fingers can manage the delicacy of making jewelry."

"It's easy, dear, once you get the hang of it," Virginia said with new energy. "First things first, we're going to need a lot of beading wire."

* * *

Eloise and Virginia threw themselves into their new project. After their morning visits with the growing murder in the garden, they returned to Eloise's cottage to work on transforming the crows' gifts. They made necklaces, bracelets, earrings, wind chimes, dream catchers, and any other trinket they could think of to make use of the endless potpourri of little tributes. The piles of bric-à-brac suddenly felt like gold as trash turned to treasure in the ladies' hands.

"A red bottle cap would be perfect here," Virginia said, finishing a charm bracelet.

"I saw a Dr. Pepper bottle cap in the pile by the nightstand," Eloise said.

Cottage #6 had become a full-steam found-object jewelry factory, with President Eloise Goodwin and Vice-President Virginia Ortega crafting lovely little works of art they called "Baubles of the Keepers of the Night Garden." The ladies gave their handmade goods to the residents and staff of Lionheart Park. Nurse Kim loved her "silver-and-jade" necklace. Clayton wore his rugged leather-and-stone bracelet at all hours. Dr. Flowers felt touched when given an elaborate decorative chain for his antique pocket watch. Even Manager Vicki enjoyed a silk headband overlaid with sparking pebbles and polished beach glass.

All twenty-eight residents had at least three pieces from the collection, some requesting more to send home to their grandchildren. The inventory of their endeavor soon dwindled, much to Eloise's delight.

Still, the crows kept delivering tributes to the rattan doormat of Cottage #6. Each morning there sat a newly scattered pile of debris for Eloise and Virginia to work with. It gave them a renewed sense of purpose and the satisfaction of knowing that something they created had value to others.

Of all the pieces from their vast collection, Eloise held onto her first and most valuable creation – a blue-and-gold bracelet she and Bernardo made together. She wore it day and night, fastening it to her right hand, for it was the hand she used to feed and pet her feathered friend. After wearing it for a week, she woke one morning to find Bernardo sitting on the bed, his wounded wing brushed against their bracelet. Eloise couldn't be sure if he slept there out of affection for her or out of a sense of territory for the pebbles he'd placed on her arm. It didn't matter. Eloise felt comfort in sharing a bed.

Cursed with never being able to conceive, and having grown apart from her adopted son Oscar, Eloise saw this curious crow, cradled in the crook of her arm while she slept, as the closest she'd ever get to feeling like a mother again.

6

Clayton stepped out of Cottage #10, his home located directly behind the central house, with a pail of rags, sponges, cleaners, and polishes. He headed to the old horse stables where Marilyn awaited another afternoon of pampering. Eighteen residents were already there, sitting in lawn chairs at the entrance to the stables with cups of tea, mugs of coffee, bowls of oatmeal, and assorted day-old Krispy Kreme donuts. Their mid-morning social revolved around Clayton and his classic car, and they expected another pleasant day of conversation reminiscing about their years before retreating to a retirement home on the cliffs of the Pacific Ocean.

Just as he did the day before, and all the days before that, Clayton obliged them with stories from his "best times." He revisited his tours of duty in Vietnam and Korea, his re-entry into civilian life as an engineer for General Motors, and his post-retirement job as a Sales Supervisor for the Hemmit Auto Group family of car dealerships in San Luis Obispo. The residents had all his stories memorized, yet found comfort in his joy in retelling them. It felt like classic television reruns brought to life.

Eloise, Virginia, and Helene joined the group after their secret sunrise rendezvous with the murder in the garden, with Bernardo left behind on the rear patio of her cottage. It pleased Eloise to see the crotchety old man wearing one of her bracelets as he cared for his precious burgundy-and-white Cadillac Eldorado Biarritz. She knew he adored the trinket, though he'd never admit it.

"A lot more people here than usual," Helene said, setting up her patio chair.

"I've seen them all here before," Virginia said.

"Sure, everyone here comes from time to time, but never all at once."

"They're wearing our jewelry. Margaret Thornton is wearing all five pieces we gave her."

"Yes, a bit much so early in the morning."

"It's the jewelry that brought them together," Eloise said. "The Baubles of the Keepers of the Night Garden have given us all something in common, like members of an exclusive club."

"The Crow Lovers Club," Virginia said.

"I don't know about all that," Helene said, "but it's nice to see most of us here together instead of stuck in our rooms with the curtains drawn." She thought of her many years as a shut-in, and how Bernardo and the other crows brought her out into the sun again. Perhaps Eloise was right. Perhaps the birds' gifts had played a central role in gathering them.

"It's certainly nice to see you out and about, Helene," Virginia said, pouring them cups of coffee from a tall, plaid thermal bottle.

"It's nice to be seen, I suppose."

The three ladies sat a few feet away from the "show." They listened to Clayton's life story and shared chapters of their own lives, sipping coffee and nibbling croissants as they strolled through memories of youth.

Clayton tuned his car radio to Rock Oldies 1290 AM, a local station of classic tunes from a time when "rock" music simply meant a guitar and an upbeat tempo. Dion and The Belmonts performed "A Teenager in Love," dripping with romance, much to the nostalgia of the residents.

"Sounds good, don't it?" Clayton asked. "It's the original Wonderbar AM radio with factory-installed four-by-ten speakers all around. Come, take a look."

Eloise alone had yet to get a tour of Marilyn's sound system, considered state-of-the-art in 1959. She agreed that the music was rich and vibrant for a set-up that had long been outpaced by modern technology. Peering into the car at an awkward angle, holding her coffee with Splenda and heavy cream, she fumbled for a moment and spilled a scattered splash onto Marilyn's driver's door and a portion of her hood.

Known for his quick temper, Clayton's abrupt, extreme reaction took no one by surprise, but was no less disturbing to witness.

"Eloise, you dolt!" he yelled. "The one time you take a peak into Marilyn and you pour hot coffee everywhere? Did you leave your brain at home? What the hell is wrong with you!"

"I apologize, Clayton," Eloise said, sincerely sorry for soiling his most valued possession. "I'll clean it up."

"No, I will! Knowing you, you'll only scratch the paint! Step away from her!"

"There's no need for that tone..."

"I believe there is a need!" Clayton said, his eyes wide. "You clearly don't have the respect needed to appreciate an Eldorado Biarritz! Sit down! Now!"

"I'm truly sorry," Eloise said, muttering to herself.

Clayton tried to stem his frustration, his infamous short fuse having caused him grief since he was a boy, but the harsh words kept tumbling out. "I was a fool to think you were worthy of being anywhere near Marilyn, much less craning your bony neck inside for a peek. I can't believe I trusted you."

All eyes on her, Eloise scooted back, regretting the decision to finally venture away from her corner of the village and socialize with the other residents. The jewelry that she crafted, that everyone seemed to enjoy, gave her a false confidence. She never should have strayed from her garden.

"Calm down, Clayton," Helene said, her voice of reason ignored.

"It's no wonder you hang around statues!" The old man's stare never left Eloise. "They're the only ones who can tolerate you!"

"That's enough, Clayton!" Helene said. "You're behaving like a drunkard!"

"Go be with them!" Clayton continued, pressing his palm to Eloise's shoulder. "And don't come back until you've learned some manners! You clumsy, mindless cow!"

Out of confusion and fear of becoming the next target of his wrath, the gathered residents sat in silence as Clayton dressed down one of their own.

"Please, Clayton, let me..." Eloise said, grabbing a rag.

"I said get away you ignoramus!" Clayton snatched the rag from her hand and threw it to the ground.

As the hostile words left Clayton's mouth, he saw the other residents staring in shock and disappointment. It felt like glancing at a grand mirror to see what a beast he had become in such a short time. He realized he'd been neglecting his pills and let his tempest of emotions spiral again, with poor Eloise enduring the brunt of his fury. For his unruly outburst, and for the deflated look on her face, he suddenly felt deep remorse and sorrow.

"Eloise," Clayton said, his voice trembling. "Please forgive me... I'm the ignoramus... I mean..."

Before Clayton could think of the right words to make amends with his friend, a kind-hearted woman who'd shown him only respect and friendship over so many years, he spotted something alarming in the corner of his eye.

Perched in the Live Oak and Gold Medallion trees that lined the driveway leading to the central house, a murder of crows a hundred strong settled among the branches, their black marble eyes fixed on the skinny old man beside his flashy machine, their numbers so great as to make the trees block out the mid-morning sun.

Clayton didn't know why they sat there staring at him, but instinctively felt his boorish behavior was to blame.

"Eloise," he said, careful not to raise his voice. "I'm sorry for..."

All at once, the crows leapt from their trees and swooped down toward the old man, their caws and shrieks drowning the sounds of the ocean and the passing traffic on James Way.

The residents knelt on the ground, covering their heads with their hands. Virginia and Helene dropped to the ground as well, pulling Eloise down with them, though she protested.

"Leave him alone!" Eloise cried, remaining on her feet.

Surrounded by a cloud of black dread, of feathers flying and beaks and bills aimed at Clayton's skull, the old man ran for cover behind his Cadillac. In seconds, the classic car was covered bumper-to-bumper with immense crows, all screaming with beaks wide open. They jockeyed for position to accost the man who had dared violate their caregiver, jabbing their sharp bills at his head. Blood trickled from Clayton's face as he curled into a ball on the ground while the crows drenched Marilyn with an immeasurable spattering. The classic car went from wine red to guano white in a matter of seconds.

Eloise ran to Clayton at the front of the car, shielding him with her outstretched arms.

"Leave him alone!" she yelled.

With Eloise blocking their attack, the crows ceased their collective battle cry and returned to the tops of the oaks, awaiting another opening.

"What is this?" Clayton asked, short of breath, not sure what was happening or why. "Are these goddamn birds protecting you?"

"They made your bracelet," she said to Clayton and to the terrorized onlookers. "Your necklaces, your charms, your rings. They're watching over me. That's all."

Clayton slowly rose to his feet. Eloise wrapped her arms around him as if claiming him off-limits. Seeing this, the crows dispersed, satisfied that the conflict was over.

"What the hell was that?" Clayton asked with a gasp, desperately trying to catch his breath.

"It's a long story," Eloise said. "Just mind your manners and they'll keep their distance. And I am truly sorry about the coffee."

"Apology... not accepted," the old man said, waiting for another assault. Both remorse and fear tripped off his tongue. "I was the fool, not you. Sometimes, I lose control."

"So do I."

"I... I can see that." He looked to the trees, swaying in the breeze, alive with rage.

Eloise did her best to sound like a confident "birder" like Helene, an expert at crow psychology. Sadly, she realized she knew nothing about the territorial nature of the flock and how they regarded her as one of their own. She didn't know how protective they could be, and for the first time since meeting them in the Night Garden, she feared them.

Virginia was right all along.

"Murder" turned out to be the proper term for the flock.

7

October normally brightened the residents' spirits as they prepared for the annual Central Coast Halloween Hop, a day-long event sponsored by San Luis Obispo County Historic Home Owners, an organization of privately owned houses of architectural renown. Among that collection of exquisite properties, Lionheart Park's central house was a gem. Built in 1901, the yellow-and-white Victorian mansion stood three stories tall, a rare height in that region of the country at the turn of the century. It held the hearts of dilettantes and aesthetes of local architecture, often featured in magazines and photography books.

The 120-year-old home's ornate design felt perfect for a good old-fashioned haunted house, if not for its sunny color scheme. It proved enough to convince Manager Vicki to enter the home in the Halloween Hop, where families from all over the Central Coast and beyond would visit the many historic homes on the local register for safe, controlled trick-or-treating. They'd come and roam the richly appointed halls of the central house, knocking on the doors of its twelve residents, before moving on to the sixteen matching cottages that surrounded it.

Halloween brought tourists to the home and along with it the fresh, new energy of small children, eager to show their adorable costumes to the beaming old folks with their ready pillowcases stuffed with candy. During those few festive hours, it felt like everyone's grandchildren came together for a grand visit.

October normally brightened the residents' spirits, but this year it brought dread.

Eloise's murder of crows didn't forget Clayton's unacceptable behavior the day she spilled her coffee. They didn't forget how almost none of the other residents came to her aide, sitting in shock in their lawn chairs as their morning show of Clayton's stories devolved into cruel conflict.

Custodian Eli felt the sharp jabs of frenzied beaks while atop a tall ladder as he hung up orange and yellow lights, large paper mâché jack-o'-lanterns, and cardboard bats suspended in stretched-cotton spider webs. He nearly fell three stories as Boxer – the largest of the murder – led a flock of bombarding ravens. Physical Therapist Billy abruptly cancelled his afternoon yoga sessions in front of the house after Butch and two dozen other rooks grabbed at the residents' hair, screeching as they circled over the crowd. Nurse Kim feared walking to her minivan after seeing Brandywine and several other House crows standing on it, waiting for her.

Only Eloise and her two morning companions were spared bullying from the birds. The staff and other residents remained indoors, once again peeking out through the curtains as the black mass hovered over the property, waiting for someone to dare step outside.

Bernardo remained with his mother, never taking part in the campaign of terror. His constant, peaceful presence gave Eloise hope, yet she still had no solution to offer.

"Vicki is talking about dropping out of the Hop," Virginia said one morning on the bench. "She's afraid the crows will attack the families."

"After all these years, I'm finally out of my house," Helene said, "and Halloween is going to be cancelled."

Eloise tossed French bread at the crows in the garden. She looked at Bernardo mingling with them. How she wished she could get him to convince his brethren to forgive everyone.

"Our secret is out, you realize," Helene said. "After the flock defended you from Clayton, all eyes are fixed on us and the birds. There are probably lookie-loos watching us now."

"They don't know about Bernardo," Eloise said. "Not yet."

"Why hasn't Vicki come to us?" Virginia asked. "I thought we'd be scolded for feeding wildlife."

"Everyone's afraid to go outside," Helene said. "Boxer and his gang sit on Eloise's roof most of the day."

"What if they try to get rid of them?" Virginia asked, fearing the worst for their little friends. "An exterminator? Someone like that?"

"They already tried," Helene said. "Eli put plastic owls and eagles all over the property to scare them off. It didn't work. He played recordings of screaming hawks in the trees. That didn't do it, either. The crows knocked down the speakers he installed."

"A custodian is not an exterminator," Virginia said. "They're gonna call professionals next, and who knows what they'll do." She looked at the crows with sympathy. "They might go straight to... you know... the last resort."

Eloise doubted things would ever come to that end, but she could see no other answer to their problem.

* * *

Edie Goodwin arrived the following morning. After several phone calls with her grandmother, long talks about the crows and how well they were socializing, she made the hour-long drive north to Arroyo Grande to not only visit Eloise but to observe the fascinating creatures she'd heard so much about.

Unfortunately, Eloise hadn't updated her on the change in the murder's behavior and disposition.

Parking her sedan in the first available spot at the start of the driveway, Edie stepped out and felt something odd in the air, as if a strong breeze had come out of nowhere and brushed through her hair. She looked to her grandmother waiting for her at the far end of the driveway, on the porch of the central house. From that distance, Eloise couldn't warn her of what was about to happen.

Boxer and Butch landed in front of Edie, blocking her path to the house. Above her, forty crows circled the sky around her car, their constant caws striking her ears like daggers. Her first thought was to call Eloise, but a canister of potato chips in hand made her fumble with her phone.

The crows swooped down at her like kamikaze pilots, their beaks aimed straight at her face. She dropped the canister, spilling potato chips across the gravel driveway.

"Gramma!" Edie cried, backing away, retreating to her car.

Eloise walked toward her, her hands outstretched. "Don't move!"

Edie heard her grandmother's command but couldn't bring herself to remain still while a battalion of crows returned to the air, gathering for another strike. She picked up the canister, only to fling it at another wave of crows, sending potato chips out into the cloud of birds.

She sat in the safety of her car and watched the vicious birds go to work on her chips. After taking a moment to catch her breath, she dialed her grandmother's number even though she stood only twenty feet from the car, inexplicably in the heart of the murder.

"Gramma, these birds are all over me!" Edie said on the phone.

"I'm sorry, butterfly, I'm still trying to figure it out."

"Figure what out?"

"The birds," Eloise said. "I know you came a long way, but visiting me now is impossible. The crows won't allow it."

"Get away before they turn on you!" Edie's first impulse was to take her grandmother from that nightmarish place. "I'm coming back tomorrow! And I'm bringing pepper spray with me!"

"No, don't do that!"

Edie didn't hear Eloise's plea. She'd hung up the phone and reversed her car back to the entrance of the property, returning to the flowing traffic of James Way. A moment later, her car barreled down the highway, away from the home.

Helene stepped off the porch and joined Eloise. They watched Boxer and Butch and their gangs of ravens and rooks picking Edie's potato chips off the gravel driveway.

"I'm sorry, dear," Helene said. "I know how much these visits mean to you. They seldom come. But the flock doesn't know that. Don't blame them."

"It's not the birds I blame."

The ladies walked to the start of the driveway, to the flock pecking potato chips and crumbs off the ground where Edie once stood.

"Clayton calls me the 'Queen of the Crows'," Eloise said. "Some queen. I should have been next to her when she got out of her car. I should have made sure this never happened."

Helene knelt and picked up a potato chip. One crow hopped to her, looking at the chip. "You think she's really coming back?" Helene asked, still observing the crows.

"I hope so."

"That's good," Helene said, forming an idea as she tossed the chip to the bird.

* * *

The following sunrise in the garden, Eloise sat with her friends on their bench. She held the end of a baguette, the crumbs falling from it onto the garden's mossy cobblestone where the morning flock gently picked it up, cawing in appreciation.

"So lovely to see Edie yesterday," Virginia said. "Even if it was from down the driveway."

"She's gained some weight," Helene said. "It's about time. She was always so skinny. I was worried for her health."

"Did you see how the others looked through their curtains at you two?" Virginia said. "They envied you."

"For what? Having a visitor or being able to go outside?"

Eloise considered the many witnesses to the attack. "Let's do it, Helene," Eloise said. "If our secret is out, we may as well spread the word."

"You sure?" Helene asked. "It's your decision to make."

"What is?" Virginia asked.

Helene had proposed a bold plan days before, one that defied everything she knew about birds. Eloise hesitated to approve. She refused to risk the other residents, the sight of Clayton's bloody face still fresh in her mind. But sitting on their eucalyptus bench that morning, the solution stared at them from the cobblestone.

The plan might work.

"We'd have to get the others involved," Helene said. "All of them."

"Involved in what?" Virginia asked, still not following her friends.

"Yes, it must be everyone," Eloise said. "We can save the Halloween Hop and the crows."

"How?" Virginia asked. "Will someone please tell me what the gosh darn plan is?"

"This," Eloise said, holding up her baguette.

8

Even before preparing for the Halloween festivities, Autumn always felt special to the residents of Lionheart Park. That October felt different, as if teetering on the cliff behind the property, ready to plummet and sink into the ocean if Helene's plan didn't work.

During the autumn months, with the changing weather ranging from hot and sunny to cold and muggy, it was normal for most of the residents to stay indoors half the day. Still, they had plenty of activities to get them out into the fresh ocean air. During any other year, some residents meandered the paths to the rear patio of the central house for coffee with Nurse Kim while others sat at the horse stables for a visit with Clayton and Marilyn. A small group of house dependents usually gathered at the end of the driveway for chair yoga and calisthenics with Skinny Billy.

That October felt different.

Since the shocking afternoon the crows attacked Clayton, the residents and staff kept to themselves, always indoors. It felt like several steps backward after finding the courage to socialize, to rediscover each other. Only Custodian Eli dared face the crows, continuing his duties, and he had plenty of scars to show for it.

From the moment they saw Clayton's tirade against Eloise, the murder turned on everyone except the three ladies that visited the garden. The residents had come to accept that they would likely miss the holiday events entirely.

Then first Monday of that October arrived.

Per Helene's plan and Eloise's instructions, all twenty-eight residents of Lionheart Park stepped out of their rooms and cottages with platters and baskets filled with breadcrumbs, roasted peanuts, and hard-boiled eggs. The entire staff – even Manager Vicki and Dr. Flowers – emerged from the rear patio of the central house with bowls of popcorn, almonds, and diced mushrooms.

Everyone placed their snacks on the ground and stepped away, ensuring that they faced the intimidating black cloud that rose from the redwoods and swirled over the property. As frightening as it felt to stand steadfast against hundreds of agitated crows, everyone agreed that the visiting kids of the Halloween Hop – their surrogate grandchildren for the day – were worth the risk.

Eloise, Virginia, and Helene were sure to be seen as well, associating themselves with the new offerings, hopefully from new friends. Eloise carried Bernardo, who seemed fully healed but still unable to fly.

"What a baby you are," Eloise told her little friend. "Am I to carry you around forever?"

"I can't believe we're actually doing this," Helene said. "How on Earth did you get Vicki to agree?" She watched everyone in front of their cottages place food on their doorsteps, satisfied that all hands were on deck.

"Eloise told her that befriending the crows would be good for morale," Virginia said. "She told her we'd have nothing to fear afterward. Right?"

"Yes, but that wasn't what got her on board," Eloise said. "I told her seeds and nuts and eggs are cheaper than hiring a team of exterminators to return week after week, and that the home's reputation would be dragged through the mud if word got out that we killed the birds surrounding the property. That waiting list of well-to-do families pinned to her bulletin board would be worthless if Lionheart's image suffered."

"It's always a wise policy to appeal to the bottom line," Helene said.

"Do you really think this will work?" Virginia asked. "I mean, do people do this sort of thing?"

Eloise wasn't sure how to respond. She knew there were rare cases of crows bonding with generous humans, but she honestly didn't know if their ambitious plan had any chance of success. The odds of three dozen people imprinting on such a large flock seemed slim, a quid pro quo of tribute gifts. Custodian Eli called it a "Hail Mary play" because, frankly, it was.

"Yes, Virginia," Eloise said, her wavering voice betraying her confidence. "It'll work."

"I was asking our resident 'birder' here."

"I think so, but it'll take time," Helene said. "Then again, this flock has always been unusual. I can't explain it, but these birds rewrite the book on Corvus behavior."

"If it takes weeks, then it takes weeks," Virginia said, confident in their idea.

"So long as it happens before Vicki pulls us out of the Hop," Eloise said. "Many of us here can't bear to wait another year to see children walk about the grounds."

"Some of us literally can't wait another year," Helene said, her ominous tone landing hard. Several residents came to mind, including the dependents in the central house.

The black swirl high above the house scattered as over a hundred crows flew down to the many plates and bowls of treats.

"I hope your brothers and sisters are smart enough to recognize an olive branch," Eloise said to Bernardo, looking down at him in her arms. "I guess I'm praying for a miracle."

On the afternoon of Halloween, after a lengthy evening phone call to explain the birds' shift in attitude and provide detailed instructions on what to do upon seeing them again, Edie agreed to return for another visit. The strategy that Eloise and Helene shared seemed unlikely to succeed, but the ladies sounded like they needed a visitor, and they did an impressive job of selling their strategy.

Following Helene's instructions, Edie returned with another canister of potato chips. As before, she parked her sedan at the start of the driveway, near the entrance. Shutting off her engine, she remained in her car as the murder of crows gathered, waiting for her to step out. She rolled down her window and tossed two handfuls of chips outside, ensuring that the crows could clearly see her face. Edie felt nervous and vulnerable keeping that window open as the crows shuffled around next to her car, picking at the potato chips. She didn't dare look directly at them but kept her face outward, accessible. In her peripheral vision, the murder looked like an infestation of immense cockroaches scrambling for greasy crumbs wedged within in the driveway's gravel.

Edie tossed out the rest of the canister and kept her face in the window as her grandmother made her way down the driveway. The swelling black mass parted as the old woman approached the car, an almost biblical sight that startled Edie.

"Good morning, Little Butterfly," Eloise said. "Thank you for coming back. Either you're crazy or I am. Shall we try Take Two?"

"So far, so good," Edie said. "They haven't tried to kill me, but then again I haven't gotten out of the car yet."

"I have a feeling you'll be alright. I prayed for you just in case."

"I've never been the religious type, but prayers are welcome right now."

Eloise opened the car door, putting Edie on the spot. Swinging the door fully open made her feel exposed with the crows only a few feet away. But her grandmother's repose and the silence of the flock put her mind at ease.

She stood from the car, gently shut the door, and walked hand-in-hand with Eloise into the crows. The birds posed no threat.

"Potato chips?" Edie asked, stunned. "Is that really what did it?"

"My flying children are just like human children. They love junk food."

"Crows don't imprint on someone so quickly," Edie said, drawing from her knowledge of Corvus. "They sometimes bond with a single person who cares for them over a matter of weeks, usually months. There's no way they've all imprinted on me over one can of chips."

"Two cans, Love," Eloise said.

"They saw me only for a minute, more than a month ago. This is... impossible."

"The crows have gotten used to us feeding and caring for them, so we have that going for us. You and I share a strong family resemblance, so there's that as well. But mostly, we have Helene to thank. She came up with this crazy idea that seems to be working."

As they approached the house, Skinny Billy stacked chairs from that morning's yoga class. He smiled at Edie, leering at her with a devilish grin. "You never told me you had a daughter," he said to Eloise. "She looks like a younger, hotter version of you."

"This is my *granddaughter*, Edie. She's one of my animal experts. She knows all about crows."

"Hell, you're in the right place," Billy said. "This place is infested with them." He offered a handshake. Edie released her grandmother's hand and took Billy's. He shook her hand for an uncomfortable minute, fixed on her like a wolf staring at a sheep. Edie had to pry her fingers from his grip. He laughed, oblivious to the tension.

Continuing past the house and the horse stables, Edie saw the other residents sitting unafraid on their porches, a few crows at their feet. Further down the path, she realized each cottage had its own little gathering of birds.

"Amazing," Edie said, breathless at the sight.

Eloise took Edie to the Night Garden, to Philomena, the statue of the tall, winged angel near her bench. Edie stared up at the sculpture, startled and amused to see an 8x10 photo of her face taped to Philomena's. At the base of the statue, crows pecked at potato chips on cobblestone.

"There's no way they fell for this stunt," Edie said. "They know that's not a real person. They're smarter than that."

"Oh, heavens yes," Eloise said. "They're birds, Love. Perhaps more than any other animal on Earth, they certainly know a statue when they see one. But eating potato chips in front of your picture for hours each day, I'm willing to bet they've gotten used to seeing your pretty face."

"My pretty face," Edie said. "A younger, hotter version of you?"

"Don't let that bother you," Eloise said with a smile. "It's the truth."

"You've been conditioning them, for the times I visit."

"'Times?' You plan on visiting again?"

Edie felt a pang of guilt from her grandmother's hopeful question. There should have been no doubt she'd come back. There should have been glorious Goodwin family reunions in the garden where they stood, Goodwin great-grandchildren running through the redwoods beyond with cousins, aunts and uncles, blood relatives and in-laws, all joined in song in the Night Garden instead of scattered, estranged, across the country.

Edie vowed in that moment that she'd never neglect her grandmother again. "You realize that because you're associating me with those chips," she said, laughing, "I now have to bring them every time I come!"

"They're on sale at Big Dollar Market for ninety-nine cents a can, Butterfly. Five bucks gets you five cans. You'll be prepared for five visits."

"I think I'll buy five *cases*," Edie said with a smile.

Eloise appreciated the sentiment, her granddaughter prepared to continue the experiment, putting herself in harm's way in order to visit her again.

"I thought you said the crows turned on everyone?" Edie asked.

"They did. But then they turned back to being sweethearts."

"No one seems put off by them. I guess Helene's plan really is working."

"Helene says it shouldn't be," Eloise said, "but it is, and I won't question why. Perhaps Bernardo talked some sense into them. They seem to value his opinion."

Sitting on the bench in front of the angel, Edie witnessed something she could never expect. She saw a single crow hop through the mass of birds to Eloise's feet, passing the ample piles of seeds and nuts, looking up to her. Eloise extended her arms. The crow toddled up her sleeves and nestled itself into her chest.

Lynn Harrod

"This must be Bernardo," Edie said in wonder as she watched the little bird respond to Eloise's every movement. "And these other are The Guardians of the Elders."

"That's beautiful, Love," Eloise said. "But we call them the 'Keepers of the Night Garden'. Virginia came up with that. It has a nice ring to it, and it removes the reminder that we're 'elders'."

"And everyone is part of this?"

"Everyone, even grumpy old Clayton and tough-guy Eli, though Skinny Billy hasn't taken to them yet."

"Skinny Billy?" Edie said. "I'm guessing he was the creep undressing me with his eyes? What does he do here?"

"Billy's our Physical Therapist. He's a hard nut to crack. I feel he hates living and working here, that he'd rather be living the high life in a big city. But I'm sure he'll come around. Everyone else did."

"You've always seen the good in everyone, Gramma. I've always admired that. The problem is that not everyone cares to see the good in themselves."

"You don't trust him? Because he hit on you?"

"No, because hitting on me disrespected you."

Eloise and Edie returned to the front of the central house in time to see the first few carloads of children arriving as part of the Halloween Hop. The little witches, pirates, vampires, and Power Rangers were welcomed by the senior citizens who longed to see youth on the grounds. Awestruck by the striking sight of the birds, the visiting families had no reason to fear the vast murder of crows that flew around the yellow-and-white Victorian manor that evening, their trust in humans on the property renewed.

At the front of the central house, within the growing crowds of tourists and their costumed children, Manager Vicki, Dr. Flowers, and Nurse Kim spoke to reporters from the San Luis Obispo Tribune, the Cal Coast Times, and KSYB Channel 6 News about the crows and the bonds they've made with the resident seniors.

"They scared me at first," Manager Vicki Carl said to a news crew camera. "I've always feared crows, vultures, scavengers like that. Fairy tales and Hollywood movies teach us to fear them. But like other classic Halloween beasts, there's nothing to fear unless you give them a reason to bring the fear."

"They're extremely intelligent," Dr. Flowers told a reporter holding an audio recorder to his face. "More than most crows from what I've been told. They remember us as individuals, even if we're bundled in coats and knit hats, with half our faces covered with scarves. Just our eyes are enough. One particular crow, they call him 'Butch,' flies to my window sill on the third floor every day at ten after two, right on the dot. I've never met anyone as punctual as that little bird. I give him a piece of my breakfast. He doesn't care what it is, whether it's a bit of scrambled eggs, a corner of toast, maybe the end of a sausage. He takes it and flies off until the next day."

"I feel safer with them around," Nurse Kim said to a Biology student blogger from California Polytechnic State University. "Imagine having a hundred flying guard dogs roaming the property." The blogger asked if Kim considered the crows tame. "No, I wouldn't say that. The residents regard them as pets, but I don't. They get along with us because they choose to, not because we've housebroken them. We've shown them we're not a threat, but we can't take them for granted. They're still wild animals."

During their televised interviews, clips of amateur footage played on the left half of the screen. The viral videos included the full murder circling above Lionheart Park, five crows landing on an old woman's cottage porch, Helene hand-feeding a raven on her forearm while two others perched on her shoulders, and Eloise showing off her blue-and-gold "tribute bracelet." She explained how her little Bernardo chose each pebble and scrap of metal for the creation.

Unlike the other residents, who planted themselves on their porches and in their open doorways to hand out candy to the children, Helene and Virginia set up a table at the end of the driveway. Along with miniature candy bars they gave out "friendship bracelets" from their surplus of crow tribute jewelry, each tagged with "Baubles of the Keepers of the Night Garden," complete with a logo of a black feather designed by Eloise. Most of the children wore their new bracelets on the spot, awestruck because they were co-created by animals.

An eight-year-old girl dressed as a black cat, her curly brown hair spilling out of her hood, approached their table with a sweet smile. "Trick or treat," the girl said. Virginia dropped a Fun Size Milky Way and an amber-and-twine bracelet into her felt-lined basket.

"I love your costume!" Virginia said. "People say black cats are bad luck. They say the same thing about crows. But I love crows! And cats! I like to think it's actually good luck to see a handsome crow with his slicked-back haircut, or cute kitten like you, crossing my path."

"I brought you good luck?" the girl asked.

"You sure did, sweetheart," Virginia said with a smile. "I can't wait to see you next year."

"Are you Virginia?"

Helene and Virginia paused, curious.

"Now how do you know my name?" Virginia asked.

"Did you see us in the news?" Helene asked. "We've all been on TV lately."

"My dad said the cute smiling lady at the table is my nana." The girl turned and pointed to a man in a gray wool coat standing a short distance away beside a BMW sedan. He smiled as he watched their meeting from afar.

"Is that your Paul?" Helene asked.

Without a word, Virginia rose to her feet, walked around the table, and wrapped her arms around her granddaughter. "Polly, you should have told me it was you under all that make-up! Helene, give her some Snickers!"

"We're all out."

"Then break out the Reese's!" Virginia knelt down to look Polly in the eye. She studied every detail of her tiny face like priceless treasure. "Look at how big you are! You were a little bun fresh out of the oven the last time I saw you!"

Paul laughed and walked up to the ladies, offering a handshake to Helene. "I'm guessing you're Helene. My mother writes about you in every letter."

"Good to finally meet you, Paul," Helene said. "Your mother talks about you every chance she gets."

"Nice turnout," Paul said, looking around at the dozens of cars and buses in the gravel driveway and the two-hundred tourists flooding the cobblestone pathways of the property. "We read all about you and your birds in the paper."

"We made the news all the way in Phoenix?" Virginia asked.

"The Paso Robles Press," Paul said. "We're moving to Paso next month. We're house-hunting there now. I figured I'd come here and show Polly her nana's 'miracle crows' everyone's talking about."

"So you'll only be forty-five minutes away?" Virginia said, still holding Polly tight.

"They have me setting up a new office there. It's a nice little town. You should come visit us once we're settled in, Mom."

Mom.

As Virginia's emotions spun, she remembered a self-help book Helene once lent her that claimed "to grow old is to grow young again," an old notion that sounds absurd at first. With each chapter, she could see why some young Philosophy PhD would think that. "The bodies of the elderly become more limited and androgynous with time," Virginia read, "turning them into toddlers who depend on others for constant care. As a lifetime of memories drift from their minds like a wilting flower's petals in a breeze, the world seems overwhelming and confusing. With no more lofty career and family goals occupying their every thought, they seek only attention and affection, quality time with those they loved."

Virginia understood the book and could recite its words as she looked upon the faces of her son and granddaughter standing before her. While she often felt like a born-again child of old age, it wasn't because of her failing body or her supposedly deteriorating mind. To Virginia and the other residents, a retirement community can often feel like an orphanage, with the orphans waiting at the window each day, longing for someone to come claim them, to include them in their lives. With Paul's news of returning to California, Virginia felt like an orphan girl rediscovering her family.

"The crows really are good luck," she said in a whisper.

"I'll even show you around the office," Paul said. "I mean, if you're interested in what brought me here."

Virginia stood and hugged her son for the first time in eight years, never wanting to let him go. Tears rolled down her cheeks as she buried her face in the lapel of his thick wool coat. "I don't care why you came back," she said. "I'm just glad you did."

9

Late November brought other visitors to the home, not from residents' relatives or curious children but from amateur ornithologists and journalists who'd heard about the wonderful flock of crows at Lionheart Park. Television crews, internet personalities, and busloads of students arrived weekly. Sundown Magazine featured Eloise and Bernardo on the cover of their annual issue, calling her the "Queen of the Crows," a moniker provided by Clayton.

California's Central Coast had always been blessed with year-round crowds of guests out to enjoy the beaches and the businesses anchored to them, a world-class wine region with bustling nightlife in nearby San Luis Obispo. Arroyo Grande and its adjacent cities never suffered a shortage of tourists, and that year was no exception. The miraculous, famous crows added to the area's newfound popularity.

Chief among the guests was Timothy Hale, a well-known author and renowned birder from Oregon. The stout, bearded man wore a gray tailored suit and a permanent smile at seeing the hundred-plus crows integrated with the senior citizens as he stepped off a bus in the driveway.

Capturing as many photos as his vintage camera could handle, Mr. Hale spent six hours touring the grounds, interviewing the residents and staff, chronicling their evolving relationships with the birds. The residents welcomed their famed guest onto their porches and into their cottages, happy to talk about their newfound love for the "miracle murder."

Upon reaching the old horse stables, Mr. Hale saw Clayton doting on his Cadillac and realized another of his passions, one that focused on vintage American automobiles in mint showroom condition.

"Cadillac Eldorado Biarritz," Mr. Hale said in awe, correctly identifying the classic car. "What an exquisite machine. Simply flawless. 1959?"

"Ain't no better year for the Biarritz," Clayton said. "You got a good eye."

"Is it all factory? Forgive me if I sound naive. It's just that the interior is perfect, the paint absolutely sublime."

Careful not to get wax on the shiny leather-and-stone bracelet Eloise made him from crow gifts, Clayton hardly took notice of the praise as he polished Marilyn's chrome bumpers. "Absolutely all factory," he said after replaying the question in his mind. "No so-called 'upgrades' here. Marilyn is a fully stock American dream. I would never besmirch her with new-fangled gizmos and whatnot."

Mr. Hale couldn't help but smile upon hearing the car's name. "Marilyn," he said, "named after Marilyn Monroe, no doubt."

"Who?" Clayton said, toying with the man.

"Monroe? The ultimate sex symbol from our time?"

"Our time?" Clayton said with a laugh to the younger man. "If you say so."

"You have exquisite taste, my friend," Mr. Hale said. "I have a few classic Caddies myself, though nothing as sexy as yours."

"Is that so?"

"Oh, yes. Back home in a converted, climate-controlled barn, I have a 1957 Series 70 Eldorado Brougham, a 1930 Madam X V-16, and a 1941 Custom 'Duchess' Limo. The limo is a 1956 certified replica, of course. Sadly, I have no relations with the Duke of Windsor."

Clayton nodded but didn't know what the nosey fat man was rambling on about. He didn't keep track of the histories or values of the vehicles Mr. Hale mentioned, or how rare any of them were. He hadn't even heard of the famous "Duchess" limo that stood as the Holy Grail of Cadillacs and one of the most historic cars in history. Clayton also didn't know that Marilyn was one of only a few hundred Biarritz soft-tops from that model year left in the world, or that there had only been ten made with original, deep-gloss burgundy paint.

Such nonsense never entered Clayton's mind, for he didn't fancy himself a curator of fine autos. He simply cherished his old convertible as the last living remnant of his glory years as an engineer, salesman, and family man, an old life where he still felt relevant and important.

Mr. Hale poked his head into the vehicle and peered through the grille at the immaculate, original engine, shaking his head in disbelief. "You ever think of selling her?"

"Ain't never heard an offer that piqued my ears."

"Does $350,000 pique your ears?" Mr. Hale asked with an amused yet serious expression. "I can make a phone call and have the money in your hands this afternoon."

Clayton never expected an offer, let alone one that approached a small fortune. He looked at the grinning fat man in his fancy suit and mirror-shined shoes, accustomed to getting whatever he wanted, with a deep disdain.

"How about $400,000?" Mr. Hale said, noticing the old man's failure to grasp the initial offer. "Like I said, it's just a phone call away."

The famous writer and collector of classic cars could never guess that Marilyn didn't get its name from the legendary movie star but from Clayton's late wife, a smart, funny woman who often wore berets and enjoyed drives up Highway One with her husband. They enjoyed the warm colors of the sunset behind the Pacific Ocean from their secluded parking spot at Sand Dollar Beach, bottles of root beer in hand. The wealthy, entitled author didn't know that Clayton proposed to his beloved in the front seat of the Cadillac as they watched the waves break in the lagoon of that desolate beach, or how the world fell away around them as she said "yes," accepting the modest silver engagement band from his shirt pocket.

Mr. Hale would never realize that the real, flesh-and-blood Marilyn Simonian-Cooper died of breast cancer so many years ago, and that this ostentatious car was all Clayton had left of her that was still "alive."

"I'm gonna hafta say no, Chief," Clayton said to the shock of Mr. Hale.

"I'm offering you nearly half a million dollars," Timothy Hale said, puzzled.

"And I'm offering you a handshake and a 'good day,' sir."

Mr. Hale stood speechless, unable to comprehend the rejection. "There's no need to be rude."

"I've been told that all my life," Clayton said. "But don't confuse a 'no' with me being rude. I heard your gracious offer and I declined, and that's all there is to say about it."

Embarrassed and taken aback, noticing the awkward expressions of the onlookers, Timothy Hale straightened his tie and placed his business card on the windshield of the Cadillac. Left to his research into the Lionheart Park crows, he walked away, sure that the difficult old man would come to his senses and call him to negotiate the next day. From his experience, the stubborn hold-outs always did.

Instead, Clayton promptly removed the card and flung it into the dirt of the horse stable, the generous offer never once tempting him.

Twenty feet away, in a lawn chair with a group of residents, sat Skinny Billy. He'd witnessed the exchange between Clayton and Mr. Hale in its entirety, educating him on the value of the old convertible. He always knew Marilyn was a beautiful classic but had no clue as to her worth.

Ensuring no eyes were on him, Billy knelt down and picked up Mr. Hale's business card.

After the most successful and enjoyable Halloween Hop the residents could recall, they looked forward to Christmas and the Winter Solstice Festival, the other annual event that the San Luis Obispo County Historic Home Owners proudly co-sponsored. With their opulent homes festooned with colorful lights and extravagant displays, it proved to be another tourist draw during a season of much celebration.

By mid-November, with Christmas only weeks away, the residents and their feathered neighbors had fully embraced each other. Butch and his twenty Rooks bypassed the Night Garden and visited Helene's porch each morning, treating her to up-close birdwatching. Brandywine and a dozen other House crows followed Virginia as she walked three laps around the property per Dr. Flowers's orders. Boxer and his gang of Ravens formed a bond with Clayton and his daily offerings of mini omelettes, circling him at the horse stables, somehow knowing that the long, shiny machine was off-limits. Such respect for Marilyn gained the old man's affection.

If only their human counterparts were so considerate of others' feelings.

On an overcast Friday afternoon, with storm clouds gathering overheard, Skinny Billy led a group of residents to the front of the central house for their daily session of Chair Yoga. If they timed it right, they might get a decent workout before the rain poured down.

Billy and his seniors carried folded chairs out to the gravel driveway, passing Clayton and his Cadillac. Whereas his fellow residents saw their friend's car as a source of pride and spirit, Billy saw an immense sack of money sitting on four whitewall tires, unguarded nightly in the horse stables.

Groundskeeper Gunther and Custodian Eli stood nearby, waiting for the group to pass before they could cross the path and tend to their duties of trimming the hedges and fixing a busted sprinkler head. Dr. Flowers always insisted that the staff wait for any passing lines of seniors, taking the moment to greet them with pleasantries like "Good morning" or "Great day for a workout."

"You guys know what that old crate is worth?" Billy asked as he passed the two men, keeping his voice low. His coworkers shook their heads. "It's worth a lot more to guys like us than an ignorant old man like him. At least we got years ahead of us to spend that kind of cash." Billy continued to the driveway, most of his class a few paces behind.

Clayton's heart fell out of his chest when Billy carelessly nicked Marilyn, the legs of his folded metal chair scraping the car's driver's door. Luckily, the five coats of vintage burgundy paint prevented any visible damage, though it was hardly any comfort for Clayton.

"Watch yourself, Billy!" Clayton said, tossing his waxing rag to the ground.

"Didn't see it," Billy said, dismissing the old man.

"Didn't see it?" The old roughneck's fuse was lit and burning fast. "You didn't see Marilyn sitting right there? She weighs two-and-a-half tons! She's nineteen feet long, shiny, and red! Kinda hard to miss her!"

"I said I didn't see it."

"Half of us are half-blind and we see her just fine! Do you need glasses for that thick skull?"

"No harm done," Billy said, stopping to ensure the old man could hear him. "Control yourself now."

"Me? Control myself? You're lucky your fool move didn't cause no damage. If even one flake of paint falls from her door panel in the next week, I'm going to Vicki and demanding your job!"

The angry old man may have sounded hasty and judgmental, but this confrontation between the two was not without precedent.

Known by all, Clayton and Billy never enjoyed a jovial friendship, the old man feeling only contempt for the younger man's questionable qualifications and thoughtless decisions. He had no respect for Billy's half-page resume as a Physical Therapist and voiced that concern often. The rumors of Billy's frequent visits to casinos and the Atascadero Pawn and Loan with residents' belongings seemed on point, something he always urged Manager Vicki to consider. On several occasions, he pointed out that Billy often worked the seniors too hard, took trays of food home from the nightly dinners, and expressed no remorse whenever a complaint was filed against him.

Such complaints filled Billy's personnel file.

Clayton knelt beside his treasured car and spied a one-inch scratch in the paint, barely visible. "Look at what you did!"

"That'll buff out easy. It didn't even get through the paint."

"How about we trade your excuses and amateur observations for a simple apology? You think you can muster that?"

Billy never apologized for any of his alleged transgressions. He viewed apologies as forced confessions and signs of weakness, and he would never tolerate the residents seeing him as weak. "It was an accident, Clayton. Calm down."

"Alright, I'll say it for you, boy," Clayton said, making no effort to contain his flurry of rage. "I'm sorry about scraping your car! I'm sorry I was a fool who didn't know my ass from a hole in the ground! Sorry I didn't apologize the moment I realized what happened! Sorry that the home hired a cheap rookie straight out of community college with only six months of actual goddamn experience!"

Affronted, Skinny Billy tossed his folded metal chair to the ground and approached the old man, his chest puffed out like a schoolyard bully. In that moment, Clayton Cooper didn't feel like an 85-year-old man in a retirement home. The adrenalin from his rage gave him the sensation that he could whoop this young man in a fight, deservedly so.

That same moment, Billy Fykes didn't feel like the Physical Therapist of Lionheart Park, responsible for the health of his clients. The embarrassing scene made him feel he'd been challenged and that he'd be justified if he were to shove the frail, irate idiot to the ground, knocking some sense of reality into him.

"You need to calm down right now," Billy said, his face inches from Clayton's. "Don't forget who's in charge of who."

"I ain't in your yoga class, boy," Clayton said, "or your made-up version of tai chi jibber-jabber. I ain't yet no invalid that needs a runt like you to wipe my ass." Still fixed on Billy, he eyed the young man's clinched fists, trembling at his side. "What're you thinking, tough guy? Gonna hit me over the head with a chair like some ridiculous TV wrestler?"

"I happen to have a chair right here," Billy said.

Before the tension could escalate further, Nurse Kim ran out of the house to them, placing herself between the two men. "Both of you need to stop acting like children!" she said in her thick Hmong accent. "Act your age, Clayton! And you, Billy, act like a professional! Both of you should know better!"

As the two men faced each other, Billy spotted Manager Vicki and Dr. Flowers watching from the front door of the house. He returned to his chair, folded on the ground, picked it up, and continued to the driveway. His yoga class stood staring, wondering if that was the end of the incident.

Nurse Kim focused on Clayton. "It was an accident, Clayton. If we need to call a professional to fix your car, we'll pay for it."

"You're goddamn right you will," Clayton said, struggling to control his emotions, swirling like the coming storm overhead. "And don't sound so magnanimous about it. You'd be paying for it out of the money I pour into this place each month. It's a lot of dough, in case it slipped your mind, and it pays your salary and unfortunately his."

The yoga class set up on the gravel driveway in front of the central house. Billy sat in his chair and faced his seniors, leading them in stretches and breathing exercises while synthesized new age music drifted from his iPhone.

In contrast with Billy's abstract, soothing harmonies, the Cadillac stood immaculate as always behind the class, as if mocking him.

Clayton and Nurse Kim felt relieved that the scratch was minor. The residents felt relieved that the conflict didn't result in violence. Groundskeeper Gunther and Custodian Eli tended to their duties, an awkward silence about them after their friend was dressed down before the seniors and management.

Billy didn't feel relief. He saw an insubordinate old man who had the audacity to humiliate him, taking him down a peg in front of old fools who talked trash behind his back. He saw his superiors shake their heads in disappointment while his peers turned away out of embarrassment.

More than ever, Billy saw an easy $400,000 payday parked in the horse stables.

In his mind, Billy quietly thanked Clayton for making his risky decision easy.

10

"When did you resign?" Billy asked, dealing a new round of cards, the flick of the deck obscured by the rain outside.

"This morning," Eli said. "I got another gig lined up in Santa Barbara. Vicki's got a new guy coming in on Monday to take my place. He can have fun unclogging toilets plugged with paper towels and newspaper and shit all day long."

Billy, Eli, and Gunther played poker in Billy's cottage behind the stables. After an hour of small talk, two cases of cheap lager, and the constant pattering of rain, the conversation caught up with the times.

"Wait, so you're not coming back next week?" Billy asked.

"Today was my last day. You didn't see the cake?"

Earlier that day, Virginia made a sheet-pan carrot cake with cream cheese frosting – Eli's favorite – and took it to the back patio of the house for everyone to share. She wrote "Good Luck Eli" in orange frosting on top.

"The woman knows how to bake," Gunther said.

"I guess, but she's still a dingbat," Eli said.

Billy thought about this news. "I saw the cake, but I didn't know 'good luck' meant you were leaving, Eli."

"Yeah, well, now you know. I'm leaving tonight."

"Damn, this works out perfectly."

"How's that?"

"You saw what happened today with me and that dumb ass over the car."

Gunther and Eli weren't sure what to say, simply nodding that they remembered the confrontation well.

"Old man put you in your place," Gunther said, popping open his fifth beer. "That's what I remember."

"The Billy Fykes I know would never put up with that," Eli said with a laugh. "We was waiting for you to teach him some manners."

"Right?" Billy said, incredulous. "I mean, the old coot overreacted and made me out to be the fool!"

"You got fifty years on the guy," Eli said, "but you let him sweep the floor with you."

"Hey, what could I do? Not everyone has a 'gig in Santa Barbara' to fall back on. What is this gig of yours, anyway?"

"Repo work."

"Oh man, this is perfect," Billy said, nearly salivating from the thought. "It's like it was meant to be."

"What the hell are you talking about?"

"I'm talking about Timothy Hale."

"Who?" Eli asked.

"That fat guy in the suit who recorded all the birds and residents," Gunther said. "Everyone kept talking about him, kept mentioning his name like he's a rock star."

"That's because he is," Billy said. "Timothy Hale. You're telling me you never heard of him before today? The guy's written fifty novels! Hollywood makes movies from his stuff. He's loaded to the gills! And he wants that old Caddie."

"Yeah, I heard some of that," Gunther said. "Clayton made him the fool, too."

"Did you hear the part where Hale offered four-hundred large for that crate?"

Gunther and Eli sat in silence, asking for cards as their hand played out. They knew where Billy was going but were hesitant to pursue it.

"I'll take two cards," Gunther said.

"Three," Eli said.

"Don't do this!" Billy said. "Don't act like you haven't thought about it before. You know what I'm saying. These old geezers only got a few years left, and their rich ass families don't give a flying fig if they're here or gone."

"The way I hear it, Clayton's family ain't rich," Gunther said. "And all his money is tied up in this place."

"Whatever," Billy said.

"You wanna boost the old man's Caddie?" Eli asked, breaking all pretense.

"And you don't? Come on Eli, you used to jack Lambos and Porsches in The Bay before you started fixing sinks and toilets in this dump. This should be easy money for you. Don't tell me the idea hasn't crossed your mind."

"Sure," Eli said. "But if Vicki found out..."

"She won't! You're leaving, remember?"

"So?"

"So, Gunther and I will play board games with the house residents while you take care of business. It's a nice, neat alibi. We meet up later and split the four-hundred."

"Count me out," Gunther said, folding his hand. "Forget it, I didn't sign up for this. I'm just fine right here, watering azaleas and planting snapdragons along the drive, with a cool ocean breeze and everything quiet. Unlike you two, I got kids to feed. I don't need a rap sheet, thanks."

"Must be nice, not needing $133,000."

"Like I said, I didn't sign up for this."

Billy couldn't believe his friend's reluctance, which he saw as cowardice. "The hell with you, even better," he said, his excitement building as he pictured the money in his hand. "We'll split it two ways. You in for two-hundred grand, Eli?"

"What if we go through all this trouble and your famous writer says he ain't interested in a hot car?"

"What if I already called him?" Billy said, a grin stretching across his face. "What if I called him the moment he got back on his bus? I might have told him I overheard his conversation with Clayton, and I could find a way to get him that damn car. What if he said 'yes' and that he had ways of covering the trail?"

"He said that?" Eli asked, curious.

"The man has thirty other priceless cars in his climate-controlled barn. How do you think he got them? The classifieds? You think he strolled onto corner car lots with his checkbook? The One Percent don't live by the same rules as everyone else. The man has connections. We'd be protected."

Their poker hand played out with Billy taking the pot, fanning a Full House of Queens over Jacks onto the table.

"See, I'm a winner, Eli," Billy said. "I strategize and think ten steps ahead. This idea didn't just pop up today. It's been simmering in my mind for the past year."

Custodian Eli Hyde tossed his losing cards back to Billy. He ran through the scenario and its possible outcomes. With a rich prick like Hale covering for them, it seemed like a quick and easy payday.

"You guys might be good," Eli said, "playing bingo and Scattergories with the residents, but what about me? The car goes missing the day I leave? Kinda obvious, eh?"

"It'd be your word against senile old coots," Billy said. "And you'd be wearing this." Billy reached behind him and pulled open the top drawer of his bureau, producing a black ski mask. "It's an extra layer of precaution, unnecessary really, because you'll be doing it at midnight when everyone is asleep or playing games with us. No one will be around."

Eli turned the idea over in his head. As Billy said, no one would be outside at that hour, and by the time anyone realized the car was gone, Eli would be two hours south at his cousins' salvage yard in Ventura. "Where's this guy live?"

"San Francisco."

"Then he'd have to come to me for the car," Eli said. "I sure ain't showing my face anywhere near The Bay with a hot Caddie. This writer of yours, or one of his guys, would have to come to me."

"Done," Billy said. "You got a place to stash the car?"

"I can come up with something."

"I figured you could."

"But he'd have to bring cash," Eli said. "Nothing over fifty. I don't want to see a single Ben Franklin in the stacks."

"Done."

"Alright," Eli said. "I guess it is done, or rather, it will be done."

Billy shuffled the deck and dealt a new hand. "This'll be the last hand. Gunther and I need to head to the house for Scrabble and Pictionary. Let us hang out with them for a while. Don't jack sweet old 'Marilyn' before midnight. Tomorrow afternoon, we'll split the money at your place. Where're you thinking of taking it?"

"Santa Maria," Eli said, lying to his new partner. "I got a place downtown, off the 101."

"Good, that's just far enough away."

Billy handed Eli the ski mask. Gunther felt uncomfortable with the theft, but vowed to keep his mouth shut. Billy's face beamed, his plans for both revenge and profit seemingly in motion.

Eli pocketed the ski mask. As much as he loathed the residents and the fact that he was returning to his former life of boosting cars, he felt sure that this plan was solid. Like Billy, he started imagining the money in his hands. It helped to kill his hesitation and anxiety.

"Serves that bastard right," Eli said about Clayton, convincing himself that the job seemed destined to happen if only to remind the old man who held all the cards. "What could go wrong?"

Gunther knew that question never ended well.

Billy and Gunther went to the central house where several residents were still awake in the Recreation Room, reading romance novels, doing crossword puzzles, and watching an infomercial hawking immersion blenders. The seniors were startled when the two young men entered the room with board games in hand. It didn't occur to anyone that these men rarely played games with them, and never past dusk. All they saw were two fresh players for a grand game of Yahtzee or Bridge, two people full of youth and energy that the central house's dependents always yearned for.

George Collins alone questioned their presence. A former attorney from Montecito, the octogenarian lived under the 24-hour care of the central house for his failing body but still kept his sharp mind. He often spent late nights in the Recreation Room in his tucked-in dressed shirt, slacks, and leather loafers, writing his memoirs in an extensive set of color-coded college-ruled notebooks. Unlike his technophobic peers, computers didn't intimidate George. He simply felt that pen and paper stood as the purist form of expressing one's thoughts.

"It's eleven o'clock," George said. "Aren't you boys normally at a bar in San Luis around this time?"

"In this weather?" Billy said, gesturing to the growing storm seen through the windows, their panes attacked with furious rain. "My tires are bald. No way I'm driving half an hour up the 101 in this storm."

"Where's Eli? Did the storm also scare him straight?"

"Eli ain't got no car, and he's not up for games. Anything with more than three rules is too much for the guy! He knocked back a six-pack and dropped into bed."

"And Gunther?" George said. "He has a reliable truck with fairly new tires. Surely, you boys don't want to throw away an evening of wine, women, and song to play cards with a bunch of old farts in this dreary house."

"I need a new battery," Gunther said, feeling the sting of his easy lie as he spoke. "Truck doesn't start half the time. I'm not touching the wheel again until Monday when I take it to the shop."

"A wise choice, Gunther," George said. "You always were the smart one."

Gunther smiled, guilt creeping up through his intestines.

"Hey, what about me?" Billy said, forcing a laugh. "He ain't risking his bad battery, and I ain't risking my bald tires. Ain't I smart, too?"

"William, the tires on your El Camino have been bald for nearly a year," George said. "It never stopped you from painting the town red before. 'Slick treads can't stand in the way of a good time.' Isn't that what you always told Clayton whenever he encouraged you to replace those old donuts?"

Billy hated hearing Clayton's name. He hated George and his smug, know-it-all questions and the way he called him "William."

He hated everyone in that lifeless room that night. If only they'd hurry and kick the bucket and be out of his life. It didn't matter. He'd be gone soon enough. He covered his hate with a grin. "Yeah, well, Gunther talked some sense into me. You know Gunther."

"I certainly do. Like I said, he always was the smart one of your motley bunch."

Groundskeeper Gunther Groom didn't want to hear kind words from George. He didn't want to look at the warm, friendly faces so happy to spend quality time with him. Not that night. "I ain't that smart, George," he said. "But I am in the mood for cards. If I can't take people's money in SLO, I might as well take yours."

"You may surely try," George said, forgetting his initial cynicism. He pulled a chair out for the groundskeeper and swept it clean with his scarf.

At the TV in the corner, watching the miracle immersion blender turn ice, rum, and fruit into an exotic smoothie, Clayton Cooper turned around, just as surprised to see Billy and Gunther in the Recreation Room after dark as they were to see him away from Cottage #10. "Good to see you, son," he said to Gunther. He glanced at Billy, only to look away in contempt.

Skinny Billy Fykes knew that his flimsy alibi would only work if all the residents accepted them that night. If even one old goat had his suspicions, people would talk, and talk spread like a virus at the home.

"I'm leaving in the morning, Clayton," Billy said. "You'll have an entire weekend here without me. Until then, why don't you show me your poker skills? I heard you were a real player back in your day." Billy knew the old man well enough to prey on his ego.

"Back in my day?" Clayton said. "I'm a real poker player today. But I'd rather not share a table with the likes of you. I'm sure even you can understand that."

Gunther sat at a card table with George and five other residents. Billy sat beside Clayton on the couch in front of the corner TV.

"I have that blender, you know," Billy said.

"Congratulations," Clayton said. "I hear it chops, dices, and whips with ease. Exciting stuff, I'm sure."

"Give me three minutes and I can have it here for you."

"What for?"

"To make up for earlier. I was an idiot, and I never said I was sorry."

"And the blender is supposed to say that?" Clayton asked.

"It's a start, right?"

"I dunno, is it?"

"It comes with a bottle of dark Jamaican rum," Billy said. "I bet you can make a mean smoothie with that."

"I'm a gin man."

"You like Hendricks?"

"I like Tanqueray," Clayton said, his attitude falling away with Billy's attempt at reconciliation.

"Well, that I don't got, but I have Bombay Sapphire."

"Sure. That'll go a long way."

"A long way to what?"

"A long way down the road to seeing eye-to-eye with you for once," Clayton said, his grizzled scowl betraying a smile.

"You wanna deal?" Billy said, handing the old man a deck of cards.

"Fine," Clayton said. "But don't say I didn't warn you. They used to call me 'Straight Flush Cooper' back in the service."

"Let's see if you still deserve that handle."

Clayton and Billy left the couch and started a new game of poker with a few other residents. As promised, Billy left and quickly returned – drenched from the rain – with his immersion blender in one hand and a magnum of Bombay Sapphire gin in the other. No smoothies or fancy mixed drinks for them, the two poker players sat together and drank simple gin and tonic for hours.

"I misjudged you, son," Clayton soon said to Billy, the gin softening his words. "All I wanted to hear earlier was an apology. I didn't get what I wanted, and I throw a mighty tantrum when I don't get what I want."

"Some might agree," Billy said.

"And they'd be right. It was a goddamn tantrum. You didn't deserve it. Yet here you are, holding up a drink for me. Please forgive this old fool for making a scene."

"You were right to," Billy said through clinched teeth. "I was careless. I needed a wake-up call." Behind his restrained rage, a shade of guilt welled up inside Billy as the crotchety old man warmed to him. The heartfelt moment lasted only a few seconds as the thought of a $400,000 check swept it aside.

"Don't we all," Clayton said. "Hell, if I don't get my morning wake-up call, I might never wake up!"

The two men shared a laugh, Billy amused by the notion of Clayton never again rising from his bed.

Gunther sat at the neighboring table, leading an intense game of Scrabble, overhearing the phony love-in between Billy and Clayton. He thought about Eli outside, waiting for the right moment to steal Marilyn. Hopefully, the deed was done, and discovery wouldn't happen for several hours. If the rain continued, it could be half a day before anyone noticed the empty stable.

Gunther saw the joy in the seniors' faces as they played their games. He imagined their expressions turning to shock and disappointment come morning. The image hit him in the gut. Living their final years, they deserved better than to feel violated by the theft of their cherished Marilyn, Clayton most of all.

Gunther nodded to Billy, who checked the time on his watch. Surely, Eli had taken the car by then. He nodded back at Gunther as if to comfort him, *This is hard, I know, but it's going to be cool.*

A poker hand ended with Clayton winning for the fourth time in a row. Billy felt genuinely surprised at the old man's skills.

"You really are a card shark, aren't you?" Billy asked. "The rumors are true."

"All the rumors about me are true, son," Clayton said. "That includes the rumor that I gotta piss ten times a night. So if you'll excuse me, I have to see a man about a very large horse."

Clayton left the Recreation Room to relieve himself. Billy smiled and shuffled the deck.

If only Billy knew that the rumors were false, and that Clayton was not actually going to the bathroom.

As the residents of the central house played all-night games with Billy and Gunther, the residents in the outlying cottages were deep in dream, all except two.

In Cottage #6, Eloise and Bernardo tried to sleep during the fierce storm, but thunder crashed and lightning streaked across the sky, flooding her studio home with bright light. It felt like trying to sleep atop a lighthouse, her bed sitting in front of its immense, rotating beacon. Eloise never could sleep well during a thunderstorm. Her childhood fear of the booming rumble and harsh light never went away, even in her old age. She curled her body under the blankets, waiting for the sky to calm.

Bernardo stood on a wooden dowel perch Eloise made for him, mounted to the corner of her desk. He whipped his head to the windows with each strike of lightning until the moment an angry clap of thunder shook him from his perch.

Eloise laid in bed, staring in awe at her little crow flying about the room for the first time. His wing had clearly healed, he was finally ready to rejoin his brethren in the redwoods. Seeing his wings spread as he flew from wall to wall, she felt a sense of joy founded by an underlying sadness.

"When the sun comes up, and the storm has gone," she said, "we'll go to the garden, to the other birds. It's time for you to fly away."

The little crow circled the room, bumping against the ceiling. He landed on the nightstand a few feet from his mother and looked her in the eyes as if confused.

"This tiny room is a cage, and that's no place for a bird," Eloise said, forcing the words. "It's no place for an old woman, either. But you have your youth and your wings, and I can't hold you here. You belong in the trees and the sky."

Bernardo had been in Eloise's care for so long, she wondered if he'd welcome the freedom of the sky. Regardless, she knew it had to be, that it would be best for him to rejoin the flock as soon as possible even if it left her alone again. His brief flight about the room, his wings outstretched as he soared bumping across the ceiling, tormented her. She suddenly saw him as trapped, both by the four walls and her selfish needs for someone to care for. She regarded him not as a pet but as a friend, and what kind of cruel friend would she be to keep him there another moment. The guilt overwhelmed her, pained her, and she could take it no longer.

"Why wait?" Eloise said, fighting her hesitation, her need to see him sitting on her desk or nestled in her pillow come morning. "Boxer and Butch and Brandywine are out there right now, roosting in the redwoods. That's a crow's life. Why not join them now and wake up in the high branches alongside them? The storm is angry, but the trees aren't far. I'm sure they'd love to see you."

Bernardo watched Eloise peer out the window at the pounding rain outside.

He watched as she put on her parka.

* * *

Former Custodian Eli Hyde remained hidden in Billy's cottage behind the old horse stables, drinking his coworker's stock of tequila and brandy. He was supposed to creep out to the stables at midnight, donned with a ski mask and a satchel of tools, and steal the burgundy-and-white 1959 Cadillac Eldorado Biarritz for Mr. Timothy Hale. But the relentless storm and shelf of booze discouraged the plan, keeping Eli in the cottage far longer than planned.

With the time approaching one o'clock, Eli dismissed his fuzzy head and the foreboding tempest, grabbed his headlamp and tools, and made his way to the stables, stumbling and reeking of liquor along the way. He saw Marilyn sitting peacefully in her shelter, the violent storm shaking the rafters above. Like Billy had foreseen, no one was there. In the darkness and relative quiet of the stable, the mint-condition Cadillac sat undisturbed, its burgundy paint glistening from the incessant lightning.

"Easy money," he said, muttering to himself as he readied his ring of ten jiggler lock picks, a staple of every repo man's arsenal. Fiddling in the dark with the driver's door, his headlamp shining on the door lock, he soon realized his jigglers were unnecessary for the door had been left unlocked.

Shining his headlamp through the window, Eli was startled to see Clayton inside, sitting at the wheel, slightly drunk, eyes clinched shut, talking to a someone who wasn't there. The barrage of noise from the storm and the clattering of the rafters masked Eli's movements, even standing just a few feet away.

"Happy Anniversary," Clayton said to his unseen companion, his eyes closed tight as he sipped the generous glass of gin Billy had poured for him minutes before. "The storm reminds me of our night at Pigeon Point. You remember? You was so scared, and I was so full o' myself. I thought us being together would soothe your nerves, but you clung to me and we watched the sky rip open and the gods bellow to the sea. You seemed so vulnerable, so beautiful. I shoulda driven us home. I wanted to take away your fear, to be scared for you. So sorry, my love. Please forgive me, Marilyn."

Eli watched the scene unfold, the fragile old man pouring his heart out to his late wife in the car that was her namesake. For the first time, he realized why the car meant so much to him, why he doted on it and cherished it beyond any amount of money.

Eli considered walking away, leaving Clayton to his ghost, his haunted past.

Looking down, his headlamp shined on his open satchel of tools, the lock picks, the jumper cables, the small crow bar. He imagined Timothy Hale driving south to his cousin Ricky's undisclosed salvage yard with a check for almost half a million dollars – all for him – holding it out with the promise of a new life. It was a promise of one last crime that no one would ever uncover, not even the man who conceived it.

The temptation proved too great, the header of every chapter in Eli's life. His momentary morals were trampled dead by six figures of cold, hard, tax-free cash, ripe for the taking.

"To hell with Billy," Eli said. "To hell with the old man."

In the chaos of the storm, Eli whipped open the driver's door.

11

Eloise sat in bed, undecided, her plastic rain parka and boots on, staring at Bernardo on her desk. Neither of them felt tired, as if they both knew it was his last night in her care. If she waited out the storm and drifted to sleep, the two of them would go to the Night Garden at sunrise. They'd sit on the bench with the ladies, drink coffee, and eat French bread, with only one of them returning to Cottage #6.

"You can't sleep either?" she asked. "Perhaps a warm milk toddy can help me shut these eyes." She still felt unsure about saying goodbye to her friend before dawn. She sat at her desk, picked up the Princess Slimline, and called the central house. Expecting Nurse Kim or one of her aides to answer, she was surprised to hear Skinny Billy's voice.

"Unit Six?" Billy said, reading the caller ID on the house phone. "What do you need?"

"The storm is keeping me awake," Eloise said. "If it's not too much trouble, I'd like a warm milk toddy, please."

"Eloise," he said, recognizing her voice. "I can make it for you, but you'll have to come get it."

"Why is that?"

"We stop food service at ten o'clock."

"It's 24-hour care," Eloise said.

"For the dependents in the house, sure, but you're independent. And it's not like you're asking for medicine. You're asking for a drink."

"I'm asking for something to help me sleep," Eloise said. "Where's Kim?" Nurse Kim would have made her the drink and hurried it over in less time than their blasted conversation took.

"My plans for the evening got derailed by the storm, so I told Kim I'd handle the common area tonight. We're still playing games. You should come over."

"In this horrid weather?"

Billy told Eloise that he couldn't send someone to deliver food or assist her in coming to the central house for "insurance reasons." Eloise believed nothing he said and wondered why he was playing board games in the house so late on a Friday instead of closing down a bar in San Luis Obispo.

"I hear you're a genius at Gin Rummy," Billy said. "Come, show me what you got. Gunther, George, and Clayton are here, too."

Billy could have easily fulfilled Eloise's request for a milk toddy and helped her fall asleep. He could have walked the short distance to her cottage and escorted her to the common area of the central house, to the Recreation Room to play cards. Neither of those options aligned with his plan for an alibi. He needed as many residents as possible to see him at the house while Eli stole the

Cadillac. The evening started well enough with a room full of residents playing games and watching TV near him and Gunther, but most of them fell asleep or retired to their rooms, and if he dared leave the house for any reason he'd surely become a suspect come morning.

With only a few residents left awake in the common area – three men known to have Mild Cognitive Impairment – Billy's alibi grew thin. For a mature woman of 85 years, Eloise still had her full faculties. Billy needed her to upright his sagging alibi.

"Come over!" Billy said. "You can bring Barney with you."

"Bernardo."

"Of course. Bernardo. He can be your good luck charm. You're gonna need it when you play against me."

Eloise looked at her clock on her nightstand. It was one o'clock in the morning. How ridiculous it'd be to step out so late during a ferocious storm to play Gin Rummy with Skinny Billy Fykes. On any other night, she would have rejected the notion flat. But that night felt important. She dreaded falling asleep and waking up at sunrise only to have perhaps an hour of Bernardo's time in the garden before he left her forever to reconnect with his flock. Billy's all-nighter at the central house would give her a little more quality time with Bernardo before their morning farewell. It felt foolish, yet she pondered it.

"Fire up that milk toddy," she said on the phone. "I'll be there in ten minutes."

Eloise bundled herself in a long-sleeve shirt, vest, and sweater all covered by her plastic parka. She held Bernardo in the crook of her right arm under her parka to keep him dry, his little talons clinging

Lynn Harrod

to her blue-and-gold bracelet, the first and most precious piece of jewelry they made together. It felt absurd to protect a bird from the elements, even as fierce as they were that night, but she remembered that the rest of the murder sat densely packed, warm and protected, within their roost in the redwoods.

As she shuffled down the path to the central house, she soon reached a T-junction, splitting the path north to the central house and south to the Night Garden. With the rear patio of the Common Area within sight, and the Recreation Room merely a wall behind it, she could have been sitting dry at a card table with a milk toddy in minutes. Instead, standing on moonlit cobblestone path, her boots filling with rain, she felt the howling wind pull her down the south path toward the garden.

Walking in past the rock wall, the garden struck Eloise as dreary, almost sinister. She rarely entered the garden so late in the evening, and never during such harsh weather. The flowerbeds were unseen in their shadows, the little statues of children and animals sat in misery in the downpour, and the towering silhouette of Philomena stood ominously against a backdrop of a lightning-flashed sky, as if her raised wings had summoned the storm.

Eloise set Bernardo down on the cobblestone and waited for him to fly into the night, disappearing in the trees forever, an image she dreaded but knew had to be. The little black crow stood before her, staring up at her.

"I fear I've ruined you," she said. "I fear I've taken away the wild, carefree crow and fastened you to me, tamed as a common pet. How selfish I've been, and how foolish you're being." The storm shook the trees and shorn the flowers, the roar of thunder and the strike of lightning compounding their delicate moment. "Fly away!" Eloise said, shouting down at the little bird. "You're better now! You deserve better! Go on! Get away! Leave me!"

Though his wings were full and well, Bernardo didn't abandon her like she'd imagined so many times. Instead, he hopped to her feet as he'd always done, content to stay with his mother.

"Everyone leaves!" Eloise said. "Now it's your turn!"

Bernardo hopped onto her toes and looked up at her.

With a clap of thunder overhead, she kicked the little crow across the cobblestone, sending him awkwardly to the flowerbeds, a rash move she instantly regretted. She wanted to run to him, to make sure he was okay, but remained at the base of the statue, determined to return him to the roost beyond the garden walls.

With the rain pounding down, Eloise saw Bernardo stand upright from his cruel banishment and fly high above the angel, landing perfectly on the tip of its right wing.

"Go away!" Eloise screamed, waiting for him to soar into the blackened sky, the sharp claws of lightning piercing the distant hills. Bernardo flew into the clouds, swooped back down, circled the garden twice, and landed on the familiar eucalyptus Adirondack bench he and his caretaker had shared for so long. Eloise sat beside him, pulling her parka tight against the rain.

"Looks like you're not ready, either," she said, relenting. "I'm so sorry, Bernardo. Let's go get that milk toddy from Billy. We'll try again in the morning, whether or not we want to." She picked up the crow, placed him on her shoulder, and left the Night Garden.

During the day, the walk from the garden to the central house wasn't far, but within the storm it felt like a country mile. Each step needed to be a careful one – slow and firm – for fear of slipping on wet cobblestone. Returning to the rear patio, with the Recreation Room just behind it, she hesitated to walk up the steep, narrow steps or the adjacent wheelchair ramp, for both looked treacherous as streams of water cascaded down them. Both the steps and the ramp were already difficult for her by day. The sheeting rain would surely guarantee a fall. Eloise needed to enter the house through the front door.

Following the path around the north side of the house, she saw movement at the horse stables ahead. Silhouetted by moonlight, it appeared to be two people talking, the storm drowning out their words. As she approached, she realized they were screaming, cursing, throwing things.

Hidden in a long shadow, Eloise entered the stables, joining a disturbing scene.

A stocky young man in a black ski mask held a crow bar, confronting Clayton who stood like a soldier at ready by his Cadillac's open driver's door. The frail yet feisty old man held a fighting stance, ready and eager to duke it out with the would-be thief.

"That Hale fellow sent you, didn't he?" Clayton said, screaming over the rain peppering the corrugated roof of the horse stable. "He couldn't have Marilyn then, and he can't have her now! No matter if you got a crow bar or a knife or a machine gun! No means no!"

The stocky thief didn't speak. He simply stood in front of Clayton, his crow bar raised as if he were to strike him at any moment.

Behind the mask, Eli Hyde's hesitation stemmed not from fear or compassion but second thoughts. Clayton Cooper stood his ground, not to be removed by any threat. A single blow from the crow bar would likely kill the old man. Was $400,000 worth it? Eli would harbor no remorse for sending the old codger to an early death. It was inevitable and likely to happen in the coming years, anyway. "Some fools are lucky and some ain't," he thought.

But Eli had turned the page to a new chapter in his life, one with legitimate work and decent money with his cousin's repossession agency in Ventura. Did he want that new chapter to begin with murder? Would it one day catch up with him? Didn't it always?

Before Eli, Clayton, or Eloise could make a decision, Bernardo flew from his mother's shoulder and attacked the masked thief.

Clayton took that as his chance to also advance on the man.

Eli covered his head and swung the crow bar wildly as Bernardo stabbed at his skull, his little wings fluttering in a fury. Clayton clutched the crow bar, tried to force it out of the thug's hands.

Eloise could only watch from the shadows, speechless, unsure whether to run for help or distract the thief before Clayton was killed. Her impulses took over.

"Stop it!" she cried, running up to the melee.

Startled and panicked, Eli turned and swung the crow bar at her. The heavy steel bar struck her left temple solid and hard, promptly sending her to the muddy ground. The unbridled strength of that strike that would surely send anyone to the E.R., much less an old woman. Barely conscious, eyes fading, unable to move, she watched her world collapse around her.

"You're all goddamn insane!" Eli screamed. "It's just a damn car!" He snatched Bernardo from the air, tossed him to the ground, and stomped on him as if he were an oversized bug. The broken bird fluttered one wing and laid helpless in front of his mother's face. Eloise and Bernardo looked at each other, their eyes locked a foot apart, half in mud as the rain crept in sideways.

Clayton clutched the thief's ski mask, whipping it off as Eli shoved him away, sending him out into the rain to fall down a small flight of cement stairs, the ski mask firmly in his hands.

His face now exposed, the crow's talons and the old man's fingernails etched into his flesh, Eli screamed expletives as he got into the car and started the engine. Hot wiring those old classics was already simple for him, but it was made easier by Clayton's technophobic, stubborn refusal to install an alarm.

Marilyn's massive engine roared to life as Eli shifted into gear and rocketed out of the stable, down the tree-lined gravel driveway, whipping south on James Way. The throaty sound of the engine grew distant until it disappeared within the storm, leaving only the pattering of rain on the trees, the corrugated metal roof of the horse stables, and the bodies of two elderly victims.

* * *

Thirty-two minutes later, at nearly two o'clock in the wee hours of the night, Groundskeeper Gunther Groom stepped out of the central house and into the stinging rain. No longer content with supporting Billy's alibi and cruel manipulation of the dependents, he walked back to his maintenance shack, passing the old horse stables more out of curiosity than checking on the progress of the heist.

The first thing he noticed from afar was the empty stable, Marilyn long gone. Eli had succeeded. The second thing he spotted was Clayton sprawled awkwardly against the cement stairs that led up to the stable. Gunther ran to him, screaming to be heard over the merciless rain.

"You alright?" Gunther said. "What the hell happened?"

"Forget me!" Clayton said, his mind a blur. "Check on Eloise! She's hurt bad!"

Gunther bounded up the stairs to the stables, shocked at seeing what looked like a dead old woman laying beside a dying crow.

"I didn't sign up for this," Gunther said, barely hearing his own pathetic voice in the storm. "Nobody did."

12

Eli Hyde, former custodian for Lionheart Park Retirement Village, barreled south down California Highway 101 in a mint-condition 1959 Cadillac Eldorado Biarritz, a special edition high-gloss burgundy convertible with white trim and vinyl top, one of only ten made by General Motors during its golden years. The sixteen-valve V8 engine boasted 345 horsepower and 435 foot-pounds of torque, making the rare, half-million-dollar car as powerful as it was beautiful. All of those hundreds of horses worked overtime as he kept the gas pedal glued to the floor.

None of these details mattered to Eli as he gripped the steering wheel with white knuckles, sweat pooling within his palms. At half past two o'clock in morning, he didn't contend with any traffic, but raced down the highway as if gridlock would appear at any moment. He wanted to stash the car at his cousin's salvage yard before the sun and the rest of the world rose out of bed. In his frenzy of panic, the empty roads offered no comfort, their dotted lines serving as a massive ticking clock.

Eli pushed the classic car to redline, flying 110 miles per hour down the rain-beaten, coastal road. Lightning streaked across the sky with immediate thunderous booms as he sped through the cities of Santa Maria, Los Olivos, Santa Barbara, and Carpinteria, as if the storm chased him across California.

It occurred to him that a flashy vintage automobile might attract the attention of cops working the graveyard shift, especially at the speeds he was traveling, but elevating his risk of getting caught fell far from his mind. All Eli Hyde could think about was Clayton Cooper and Eloise Goodwin, two senior citizens most likely dead by his hand, their cold, drenched bodies lying on the ground at the old horse stables.

He replayed the confrontation in his mind, wondering where it all went wrong and how he could have pulled it off without a hitch. The job seemed simple enough. He'd stolen countless cars before, exotic machines with innovative security, all far better protected than the simple coupe he was now driving. He wore a mask. The horse stable was dark. Fierce rain drowned out all sound. The car's owner was a weak old man. It should have been easy to cast him aside and take his ride. The goddamn crow lady shouldn't have been a factor.

How did a simple boost turn into a double murder?

"To hell with them," Eli said, switching on the car radio. He often spat out that vulgar phrase whenever he felt overwhelmed by his own immoral actions, whenever his conscience made his head ache. He twisted the night's events to vilify his victims for they dared to stand in his way, to deny him the life-changing fortune he'd always deserved. "To hell with them all."

The car's vintage Wonderbar radio was tuned as always to Rock Oldies 1290 AM, Clayton's favorite station. Ricky Nelson sang "Poor Little Fool" and Eli couldn't help but relate to the sweet melody's protagonist, a young man tempted by a beautiful woman with "carefree devil eyes" who ultimately delivered his undoing. By the end of the classic song, its protagonist got his comeuppance and experienced the same betrayal he'd visited upon so many others.

"To hell with them all," Eli said again, shoving down all traces of guilt and remorse. The payday was enough money to wash away his sins.

$400,000.

Indeed, his pay would be the full amount, not a ludicrous fifty-fifty split. Skinny Billy Fykes may have proposed the job, but he took none of the risks. While Eli donned the ski mask and put his life on the line in a cruel storm, facing the vehicle's volatile owner in the dead of night, Billy drank Scotch, playing Scrabble and Yahtzee in a group of sleepy senior citizens with one eye open and one foot in the grave.

Eli Hyde held all the cards that night. Yes, he now had to evade a murder investigation, but he had the car. He lied to Billy about where it would be stored. He set upon taking it to the last place anyone at the home would think to investigate, having never mentioned his goody-two-shoes cousin to anyone at Lionheart. Eli remained convinced that it should be he alone who reaped the reward.

"To hell with them all."

It made perfect sense to Eli that "them all" included Billy, who would soon discover he'd receive not one penny from Mr. Timothy Hale, a man surely accustomed to ruining people's lives for his personal gain. Billy would have no recourse for getting booted from the heist's take. He didn't know the address of the salvage yard or the details of the payout.

If Billy Fykes reached out to Hale, the famous author would deny ever meeting him, much less working out an illicit deal. Dead end. And if Billy Fykes ever came to Ventura with his hand out, Eli would kill him, just as he did poor Clayton and Eloise. What's one more body? If caught, what's the difference between two life sentences versus three?

The Point of No Return was the end of that long, gravel driveway, and Eli had looked at it in the rear-view mirror with an odd sense of comfort.

"They shouldn't have got in my way," he said, his voice trembling as he scrambled to justify his vile actions. "It's just a damn car. If you're willing to die for a car, you deserve to die for a car."

After over two hours speeding through the storm, Eli reached the Beach Boyz Salvage Yard on Cortez Street in Ventura, California, just north of the 101 and east of the 232. The yard comprised a simple house centered in an automotive junkyard, a grove of Valley Oak and Red Willows fore and aft.

Ten minutes prior, Ricky Hyde received a text from his cousin Eli that simply read, "Two exits away." It was Eli's second text to his cousin that night, the first appearing hours earlier, right after agreeing to Billy's proposal over a game of poker. Ricky waited, shivering in the rain, beside a four-bay carport just west of the salvage yard's house.

Eli pulled the stunning Cadillac into the first bay and shut off the engine. Ricky checked the time on his watch: a quarter to four o'clock in the morning.

"Perfect timing as usual," Ricky said. "You're a natural, cousin."

"I suppose so," Eli said, grunting in relief that he'd seemingly made the trek without police on his tail.

"When you said it was a sweet ride," Ricky said, "I expected a Porsche or maybe a Benz, but this is a work of art, cousin, a real beauty."

"Yeah, it's pretty."

"She drives good?"

"Like it rolled out of the factory today." Eli said, tiring of the small talk.

"Who's this repo job for?"

"Some rich fat cat in 'Frisco."

Eli forced the pleasantries, not wanting to alarm his cousin. He hadn't told him that the car was stolen, or that two people were likely killed for it.

"A dealer?" Ricky asked.

"A collector."

Ricky unfurled a tarp in the carport, struggling to keep it dry within the invading storm. Replaying his cousin's response and sensing his anxiety, something didn't feel right. "Collector? Is this really a repo? Are you boosting again, Eli?"

"You're gettin' ten-grand in the morning," Eli said. "That's all you need concern yourself with."

Ricky felt like his stomach fell out. "Jesus, cousin! I thought you was going straight?"

"I am going straight," Eli said. "Straight to the bank, right after the buyer comes to collect the car tomorrow."

"Godammit!" Ricky Hyde didn't appreciate his cousin's secrecy, or unwittingly being made an accomplice to grand theft auto. "I spent ten years building this place!" He strained to be heard above the rain slamming the carport's rotted wood roof. "You better not tear it all down with another of your get-rich-quick jobs!"

"It's the last one."

"It's always the last one, cousin!" Ricky said. "At least tell me it was clean!" Eli's hesitation told Ricky everything. "Get it the hell out of here!"

"Do you know what time it is?"

"Forget it! This ain't what we agreed to!"

Ricky didn't know that Eli had spent the past two hours battling his demons, and that the demons had won. He didn't know that Eli assaulted senior citizens to get his hands on the car, or that his former employers would promptly drop his name to the cops. He concluded, however, that the hot car would bring only trouble to his family's salvage yard and wanted to cut himself loose from the fallout.

"Goodbye, cousin, and good luck with whatever trouble you've gotten into now."

"Where the hell am I supposed to go, Ricky?"

"That's not my problem!" Ricky said, barely hearing their voices in the furious storm. "Take it to Charlie's yard in Oxnard! He doesn't care if you got it from the side of the road or his mom or the President! He'll take half what you promised me! Hell, he'd do it for a case of beer!"

"Ricky..."

"You leave now, you'll be there by sunrise! Just get it out of here! Now!"

Eli draped the canvas tarp over Marilyn, walked up to his cousin, and slammed his fist through his face. Ricky fell to the wet wooden porch, blood trickling from his mouth, shocked at the violent response. It validated his instinct, screaming to him that this job could be the end for them both.

"Charlie Harley?" Eli said. "Are you out of your damn mind?"

Both cousins knew that "Charlie Harley," an ex-con who ran an illegal chop shop in Oxnard, was unreliable at best, an opportunist who would toss you to the wolves in a heartbeat for a buck or just to cover his tracks. They also both knew that Ricky was gullible, scared, but ultimately loyal, far less likely to turn over should the authorities get involved.

"You'll get ten-grand in the morning!" Eli said. "Stop being a wimp! No one knows where I am! No one followed me here! And no one knows when I'm gonna contact the buyer! We're good and clean! So suck it up and accept your check tomorrow! You're in this pit with me, so you might as well get paid, but if you wanna keep playing the Boy Scout, I'll take it all!"

Ricky sat on the wooden floor of the carport, barely making out the commands from his older cousin. "I guess I got no choice."

"I'm getting some sleep," Eli said. "The buyer is sending a guy tomorrow at noon. After that, you'll get your money and never see me again. How's that sound, Boy Scout?"

"Is that a promise?"

Eli ignored his cousin. He left the carport and walked through the rain to the modest house in the middle of the property.

Ricky rose to his feet, clutching his sore jaw. He pulled the tarp off the front of the classic Cadillac and gazed at its beauty. "You are quite the prize," he said to the car. "I hope you're worth it."

Ricky shut off the overhead light and exited the carport.

The coastal storm continued through the night, receding to a moderate sheeting of rain by morning. Ricky told himself that the buyer would surely arrive at noon, as his cousin said, and that this ordeal would soon become a forgotten day in their lives. Finally, the Hyde Family would leave their criminal past behind.

"God forgive me," he said as he walked away from Marilyn, knowing it wasn't just a simple boost. "God forgive my cousin for whatever he did tonight."

13

Eloise fluttered and squinted her eyes as she awoke disoriented from harsh overhead lights and stark white walls. Her cluttered desk, framed artwork, potted plants, and crow tribute jewelry were missing. There were no birds chirping outside, no ocean waves fading in and out in the background, no ticking of her old bedside clock. She raised her right hand to her face, relieved that her blue-and-gold bracelet still adorned her wrist.

Bernardo.

Where was Bernardo?

Where was she?

She rubbed her fingers across the bandages wrapped around her head, bringing back the frightening scene from the horse stables. Only through that painful memory was she able to deduce from her surroundings that she was now at a hospital, having no recollection of being brought there.

Eloise sat up in bed in Room 28 of the Arroyo Grande Community Hospital, a facility twenty minutes east of Lionheart Park. Sunbeams streamed through the blinds of the second-story window, casting long shadows across her crisp, white bedsheets.

"Can we turn the lights down?" she asked, speaking to anyone who might hear.

At the end of her request, she felt the touch of someone's hand.

Edie sat in a bedside chair, slumped over asleep, her fingers clasped with her grandmother's. An hour after the late night assault, she'd gotten the alarming call from Nurse Kim who'd been fully updated about that night's events by Groundskeeper Gunther. As the grand heist was exposed, Skinny Billy Fykes quietly excused himself from the home, abandoning his possessions, taking refuge at the Sea Shell Motel in nearby Grover Beach.

Eloise sat up, releasing her hand-hold with Edie after several hours joined. The movement woke Edie, who looked about the room, remembering where she was, surprised to see her grandmother sitting up in bed.

"We finally have you back," Edie said, overjoyed, her worst fears falling away. "Dr. Flowers hoped it would be this week. How are you feeling, Gramma?"

"My head feels like it's filled with concrete," Eloise said. "Can we turn the lights down?"

Edie reached for a remote tethered to the bed frame. She held down a button to dim the ceiling lights. "Should I shut the blinds?"

"Please don't," Eloise said, not wanting to lose her glimpse of the outside world. "I'd rather you opened them up."

"Are you okay, Gramma? How much pain are you in? From one to ten."

"No pain, just heavy," Eloise said. "What an odd question, Love."

"Dr. Flowers told me to ask you that when you woke up. He made me promise."

"Then you tell him I'm a soft two."

Edie smiled and raised the window blinds, letting in the early afternoon light. She poured a glass of water from a brown plastic pitcher on the sill of a wide window with a picturesque view of Arroyo Grande Creek and miles of foothill crops beyond.

"Nice place," Eloise said, "but I can't wait to get out of here. Even hospitals as fancy as this give me the willies."

"The good news is that you'll probably be discharged today or tomorrow. It's been touch and go, but you're tough for an old goat."

"Old nanny," Eloise said. "Female goats are called nannies."

"How fitting. You used to be my nanny."

"Despite my embarrassing situation, I still am."

Tracing the wires and tubes that ran from her arms and chest to the monitoring machines beside them, Eloise tried to piece together the time she lost. "Have I been here all night? When can I leave?"

"You've been here for ten days, Gramma," Edie said, careful not to appear concerned.

"Was I in a coma?" Eloise suddenly felt unwell.

"No, nothing like that, just heavily drugged, in and out. You woke up a couple of times but knocked out again, so they eased up on your feed..."

"I don't remember..."

"Doctor said you'd be disoriented. Just take it easy, Gramma. Let us worry about how long you've been here and when you can go home."

Dr. Flowers entered the room, happy to see his patient awake and coherent. "You're back! Just in time for lunch. I hear they have a boring fish sandwich with bland French fries and watered-down apple juice coming your way."

"Lucky me."

"You are lucky, Eloise," Dr. Flowers said. "You took quite a knock to the melon."

The disturbing scene from the assault suddenly zoomed into focus. She saw and felt every moment replay across her mind. "What about Clayton?"

"He left after a couple of days. He was sore and bruised all over, but he'll be fine."

"He's the real tough old goat," Eloise said.

"He insisted on walking out on his own two legs," Dr. Flowers said. "Who am I to argue? I'm only his doctor."

"Sounds like Clayton," Edie said.

"And Bernardo?" Eloise asked, picturing her little friend, helpless, broken again, fluttering on the ground in front of her.

Dr. Flowers didn't know who she was referring to, but Edie surely did. "One of his wings is broken, and one of his legs," she said. "Helene took him to the Audubon folks."

"They should've taken him to a vet!" Eloise said. "They should've taken him to you!"

"Half of the Audubon Society are vets, Gramma. Bernardo is in good hands, the best hands."

"So, he'll be alright?" Eloise asked with a tone of desperation.

Edie didn't answer. She didn't want to give her grandmother false hope. "He's in the best hands," she repeated. It was all she could think to say.

"The little crow," Dr. Flowers said, catching up. "Don't concern yourself with him right now. Focus on you. We're still waiting for some tests, but I'm confident that you can go home tomorrow, maybe even today. We'll see."

Edie clicked on the television remote control, encouraging her grandmother to distract herself and simply rest for the day.

"I'm not in the mood for TV," Eloise said.

"Well, I am," Edie said. "These past ten days haven't been fun for me, either." She took the remote and switched channels on the television, mounted high on the wall. She sped through channels, from a classic western to a home shopping show to a local news broadcast.

Eloise spotted a familiar face on the screen.

"Leave it here," she said.

"Ladies, I'll be back later," Dr. Flower said. "You have my number if you need to call me, but the nurses will be here shortly for vitals. They'll take care of anything you need."

"Thank you, Doctor," Eloise said, her eyes now fixed on the TV.

As Dr. Flowers left the room, Edie sat on the bed beside her grandmother, intent on watching whatever caught her grandmother's eye.

KSYB local news followed up on a violent scene reported over a week ago south in Ventura, one that left authorities puzzled. Portrait photos of several hardened men were superimposed on the screen beside the news anchors.

Eloise knew two of them.

Like the rest of the Central Coast, Ventura's "Beach Boyz Salvage Yard" endured the freak winter storm that broke trees in half, backed up rush hour traffic, and flooded portions of the 101 and the industrial Cortez Street. Stacks of wrecked cars were splattered with mud and debris. Nearby businesses were acres away, making the yard feel like a ravaged island. The house in the middle of the property, already a ramshackle structure, suffered further damage to its roof and rear windows.

On the morning after the storm – the morning after his cousin arrived late at night with a stolen car and the blood of two people on his hands – Ricky Hyde stepped out of the house, adjusted his faded Ford trucker's cap, and sipped a cup of black coffee. Blinded by the California sun, rising in an immaculate sky cleared by the all-night rain, he raised his palm to block the light. He went through his keys, ready to unlock the gate for their guests from San Francisco. Expecting to see the front of his property thick with mud and endless debris from the oak and willow trees across the road, Ricky was surprised to see a turquoise El Camino parked twenty feet from his front door.

Billy Fykes sat on the open tailgate of the pickup-coupe, smoking his ninth cigarette, judging from the doused butts in the mud at his feet.

"How'd you get in here?" Ricky asked, noticing that the gate remained locked.

"That old padlock of yours didn't put up much of a fight," Billy said. "But don't worry, I didn't break it. The gate is still locked nice and tight. I'm just eager to do business is all."

"What can I do for you?" Ricky asked. "Looks like you been here a while."

"I'm interested in a Cadillac," Billy said.

Ricky's eyes widened. He didn't know how to handle this stranger who knew how to overcome a Marston industrial lock. Eli had assured him that no one knew where he took the car, and that no visitors other than the buyers would come calling. This little "low-risk" heist suddenly felt like anything but, and the thin man sitting in front of him felt like trouble.

"We got plenty of Caddies here," Ricky said. "A lot of Escalades, some SRXs. Most of them are good for parts."

"I'm interested in a classic."

"Then you're in the wrong place," Ricky said, gesturing to the stacks of wrecks to the north and south of the house. "But I got a '98 Fleetwood that still runs. I'll let it go for a grand."

"How about a '59 Eldorado Biarritz convertible? I hear you got one, wine red from what I hear."

"That's a damn fine ride," Ricky said, forcing a laugh. "But you heard wrong. You want the auction house downtown. All we got here is salvage. Who the hell told I got something prime like that?"

"Good ol' Cousin Eli," Billy said, dropping all pretense. "I know he's in that shit shack behind you, and I know my Eldorado is hidden under that tarp just over there."

"What Eldorado?" Ricky said. He felt like an idiot when he turned to see that he hadn't fully concealed Marilyn with the tarp after taking a peek hours before. In the dark heart of last night's storm, he left her chrome front bumper and driver-side headlamps partially exposed.

"You may be stupid, Ricky Hyde," Billy said, "but you're bad at playing stupid."

Ricky stood silent for an eternal, uncomfortable minute as Billy waited for their charade to end. Before Ricky could think of a response, Eli spoke for him from behind the screen door of the house.

"How'd you find me?" Eli asked, shouting from inside the house.

"Your fridge told me," Billy said. "A calendar for 'Beach Boyz Salvage Yard' was on the mini-fridge in your tool shed. 'Richard Hyde Proprietor.' I just added two and two. But don't sweat it, I snatched that calendar, got it right here. It might not stop the cops from finding you, but it'll delay them a little while." Billy pulled the four-inch magnet calendar from his pocket and tossed it to the mud near the porch. "I noticed that last night's date is circled and '400K' is scribbled on it, so you might want to burn that. Could make you look bad."

Eli saw it as bait to draw him out into the open. "What happened to the old man and the bird lady?"

"Dead, probably," Billy said, having fled Lionheart Park in the thick of the night, before the ambulance and police arrived.

"You don't seem broken up about that."

"I'm not here for revenge, if that's what you're thinking," Billy said. "They were on their way out anyway, and cops don't put up roadblocks on behalf of someone whose grave's already been picked out."

"Agreed," Eli said, still not sure if he should step out of the house. "To hell with 'em is what I say."

"You got that right. To hell with 'em."

"But they were your responsibility," Eli said. "You ain't worried?"

"I'm not worried at all. I'm not the one who beaned them over the head with a crow bar."

Aghast, Ricky backed away as he pieced together how horribly wrong their heist went down.

"Is Hale coming?" Billy asked.

"He's sending a guy, yeah," Eli said. "It'll be a few hours. Around noon, I'm told. I just texted him."

"Then we'll wait together. Come out and we'll figure the details."

"How about you come in?"

"I'd rather you joined me out here."

Eli didn't trust his partner anymore than he'd trust himself if their roles were reversed. Each man clearly intended to take full payment of the promised $400,000 on its way down from San Francisco as they spoke. In the interim hours, at this desolate salvage yard behind a locked fence, the two men would decide who'd walk away with the life-changing paycheck and who would depart with less than nothing.

Ricky stood frozen on the porch of the decrepit house, coffee cup clutched tight, his back to the wall. He wanted to talk sense into the two men, but he knew them well and realized they were about to cross a frightening line. "I don't want no trouble, boys. You two work this out. No need for anyone to get burned. There's plenty of dough in that deal of yours."

"So, you told him?" Billy said with a sigh. "You two, come over here and let's talk it out. I mean, it's beautiful out here! We're completely alone! There's nothing here except mud, cars, and trees."

Billy had his hands in his coat pockets.

Eli emerged from the house with a silver pistol aimed at his partner's head. "Why don't we forget about screwing each other and go back to the original plan," he said, now standing in the shadows of the porch.

"I think the original plan fell to shit when you took off without answering my calls," Billy said, revealing a black handgun from his coat. "I think the original plan became void when you wrote '400K' on your calendar and not '200K' like we agreed. That doesn't include whatever you promised Ricky here."

The two men faced each other, guns at ready.

"I don't want any of it," Ricky said, realizing his paltry $10,000 promise was part of the grand deception. He no longer care for any share of the payday. He just wanted the tense situation diffused. "I don't want even a buck. More for you guys."

"Considering you were never part of the deal, Cousin Ricky," Billy said, "your generosity feels a little flat."

Ricky set his coffee cup on the porch railing and shuffled to the side of the house. It was then that he noticed movement in the trees across the street, behind Billy. There was something strange about them he couldn't pinpoint.

"You boys sure you weren't followed?" Ricky asked, ready to duck behind a crate when the inevitable firefight started. He imagined cops crouched in the woods across from the property, the leaves of the immense Valley Oak and towering Red Willow trees across Cortez Street rustling in the wind.

But there was no wind, and there were no cops.

Ricky realized what seemed odd about the trees. They normally stood barren that time of year, awaiting the coming of spring, but that morning they were full and lush. Peering at them, he saw the "leaves" of the trees were actually thousands of crows, their black marble eyes all staring back.

"What the hell," Ricky said, whispering to himself, the overwhelming, nightmarish sight nearly paralyzing him.

Eli stepped out from the shadows of the porch, his pistol cocked, his face finally exposed to the morning sun.

Instantly, the trees shook violently as a black cloud left the branches and swirled into the sky, circling the lone salvage yard like an immense living shadow. A murder of crows far larger than anyone at Lionheart Park witnessed swarmed above the three men.

Ricky threw all caution aside and ran into his derelict home.

Billy and Eli pointed their guns at each other, not noticing the furious birds until they were well upon them. Blinded by the attack, Eli swung his arms wildly at the birds, firing his pistol randomly into the air. Several crows fell dead to the ground, but they were only a few of the five-thousand strong, swooping toward him, jabbing their sharp beaks into his flesh.

Billy backed away, swinging at the cloud of death, shooting his gun dry as the birds clung to him like enormous roaches, digging their talons into his arms and neck, creating spigots of blood that sprayed all around.

Within moments, Billy laid still and flat in the mud – dead – his body completely obscured by the merciless flock tearing into him.

Eli bent down low, swiping at his assailants, inching toward the house for cover as his cousin did moments before. It seemed a mile away. Tramping through knee-high snow would have been easier than tramping through the blinding flurry of the predators.

Something flashed to his right, a short distance away.

Marilyn's front chrome bumper reflected the bits of sunlight that made it through the flock. The two exposed driver-side headlamps watched Eli's struggle with the crows.

In his racing mind, Eli remembered hearing how the crows always kept their distance from the vintage car. The gullible old fools at the home assumed the birds realized how much the car meant to Clayton and thus respected its space, but Eli knew wild animals weren't that intelligent. He knew it was because of that glossy burgundy paint. It scared the crows, gave them pause, like blood spilled after a predator ripped one of them open. He knew if he made it to the car and whipped off its tarp, the stupid birds would flee.

Eli turned and powered his way through the murder toward the car, losing his left eye and the tip of his nose along the way. He clutched the tarp and pulled it to the side, exposing the car's massive hood, thirty square feet of steel.

The sight of Marilyn's unique front end did nothing to deter the onslaught.

Eli tried to crawl around to the driver's door for shelter in the cab, but the dense flock denied him those last precious steps as they dug their talons into his back. He collapsed flat to ground as hundreds of beaks and bills pierced his arms and legs and jugular.

The last thing Former Custodian Eli Hyde saw as he felt the full weight of a vengeful murder of crows was Marilyn's wide, staring face looking down at a pool of his blood pouring out onto the dirt.

14

Eloise and Edie continued watching the local news, shocked at the reports of a flock of birds killing two men with known criminal records in an isolated salvage yard in Ventura.

Almost as shocking as the attack were the details of the victims.

William "Skinny Billy" Fykes was a petty thief in the Greater San Francisco Area with multiple convictions of Breaking and Entering, Burglary, Possession of Stolen Goods, and Possession of Illegal Firearms. While serving a two-year sentence at San Quentin State Prison, he studied online and became a CPT – Certified Personal Trainer – earning a six-week certificate he would later embellish as the two-year degree of a Physical Therapist Assistant.

During his time at San Quintin, Billy met Elias "Eli" Hyde, a career car thief with a history of violence. After being released from prison, Billy found work at the Lionheart Park Retirement Village in

Arroyo Grande, serving as their resident Physical Therapist. Six months later, when Eli left prison, Billy helped his former cellmate gain work as the home's Custodian.

As the news anchor described the sordid, secret histories of the two men, Eloise felt betrayed. She and the other residents trusted them, even if they didn't like them. She wondered how they could have kept their pasts so well hidden while fabricating their educations and work experience. It occurred to her how easily Nurse Kim's confidence could be earned. She often trusted her instincts over the strict protocol of the home's background checks. Ironically, Billy often teased her for being too nice.

No doubt, Billy used all his charm and guile on Nurse Kim during his initial job interview, something Eloise had mixed feelings about. Incompletely vetting staff can be risky – dangerous – as the past two weeks had shown, but Eloise couldn't fault Nurse Kim for letting her kindness cloud her judgement. Sometimes one's strength can be a weakness, and everyone at the home equally misjudged those men.

"What you are about to see is graphic and disturbing," the news anchor announced.

Grisly photos of mauled bodies appeared on the screen. Billy and Eli were not merely killed, they were eaten alive, their bodies nearly skeletonized by five-thousand wild scavengers.

"How could they do this?" Eloise asked. "Why would they?"

"It's simple, Gramma," Edie said, barely believing her own words. "Crows communicate quickly. Within an hour, the entire flock knew what happened, and you know more than anyone how protective they can be."

"It's my fault," Eloise said. "I got them attached to everyone. I thought I was taming them. Imagine, me taming a hundred crows. What a fool I was."

"Word must have spread to a full-fledged roost in the area because witnesses say thousands of birds descended on that junkyard. That nightmare sounds like a helluva lot more than your little flock."

"You knew," Eloise said, realizing her granddaughter was aware of details on yet the TV news.

"I knew," Edie said. "I read about it last week."

"And you didn't tell me?"

"I didn't want to upset you," Edie said. "You're still in recovery, Gramma. We don't have all your tests back yet. We don't even know if you're being released today."

The follow-up news coverage continued with Richard "Ricky" Hyde, cousin of Eli and owner of the salvage yard, a legitimate business owner with no prior criminal record who claims to have been blindsided not only by the attack but his cousin's plans. He survived the incident, holed up in his house as it was bombarded for over an hour by the relentless birds. He called the police once the attack ended, after ensuring that the birds had left.

"They're going to piece together that those were our crows," Eloise said, suddenly feeling a deep pit of dread in her stomach.

Edie couldn't argue with her grandmother's logic, but she needed to keep her calm and positive for now. "What are they going to do? Prosecute a flock of birds in court? All you need be concerned with is that you were here with me, convalescing in this room, and that those men were responsible for putting you here. I promise, I'll make sure the police make those connections, Gramma."

"Thank God Bernardo wasn't there."

"He may not have been there," Edie said, "but all those birds were there for him, and for you."

"And poor Clayton." Eloise replayed her granddaughter's summary. Everything she said made sense, yet she still feared the worst. "I want to see my friend."

"I can call Clayton if that would make you feel..."

"I want to see Bernardo."

Edie felt helpless, unsure of how the next few days would play out. "In time," Edie said. "You need to rest now."

15

The Valley Oak and Gold Medallion trees that lined the driveway of Lionheart Park were decorated with Christmas lights, as were the Australian Willow and Raywood Ash trees that dotted the sprawling property, the festive holiday only a week away.

From her hospital bed, Eloise could see the decorations in her mind. Virginia called her nightly to tell her – in great detail – about the preparations they made for the coming Winter Solstice Festival and how fifteen busloads of tourists were scheduled to visit on the first day alone. Reports of the Ventura attack did not deter fans of the "Lionheart Crows" nor the legions of curious tourists. This Christmas would prove to be their biggest yet.

Though Eloise's test results were inconclusive, they showed no serious or permanent brain damage. After intense physical therapy and counseling, Dr. Flowers hesitantly released Eloise after another

Lynn Harrod

week, on an early Monday morning, if only because he could continue monitoring her at Lionheart.

Eloise returned home in the backseat of Nurse Kim's minivan with Edie sitting at her side. During every moment of that twenty-minute drive, she watched the trees and the skies for her beloved birds but saw none. She imagined them migrating south to avoid further trouble, a human cowardice she knew birds didn't share, even ones as smart as hers.

Still, she hoped to continue seeing only clear skies.

On Edie's urging, Eloise refused to dwell on the pending investigation. She didn't burden herself to think about the perceived image of the home after social media suggested that their famous crows were involved in the bizarre, brutal double-murder in Ventura. All she thought about were her original birds – Boxer, Butch, Brandywine, and especially Bernardo. She could never forgive herself if the city exterminated the crows like diseased, deranged vermin.

"Everyone's looking forward to seeing you again," Nurse Kim said in her thick Hmong accent. "Expect a little celebration. Virginia made you a triple-layer rum cake."

"I don't much feel like celebrating," Eloise said.

"I'll eat your piece," Edie said, her attempt at lightening the mood.

"I think you might change your mind once we get there," Nurse Kim said. "No one blames the crows. I certainly don't."

"Bless your heart, Kim."

"If a dog killed a burglar to protect his owner, people would understand. This is no different."

But this was different.

Eloise knew the crows flew far past protection. She knew they were intelligent enough to seek revenge.

Nurse Kim turned off James Way and drove down the home's long, gravel driveway, parking in front of the central house. As she predicted, the residents had set up tables and chairs in the yoga area, with "Welcome Back" balloons shaped like butterflies, bees, flowers, and – of course – birds.

Eloise stepped out of the minivan to great applause as her fellow residents surrounded her. Virginia led the crowd, embracing Eloise before she could take two steps. A three-tiered rum chocolate cake sat on a table next to a modest spread of submarine sandwiches and cups of punch.

Dr. Flowers, Manager Vicki, and Groundskeeper Gunther stood nearby, happy to see that she seemed healthy and aware. There were rumors of depression and anxiety, and they felt determined to counter them with a warm welcome.

Clayton Cooper didn't rush to the minivan like the others. He stood next to his Cadillac at the old horse stables, waiting for the many well-wishers to have their moments with their returning friend. The relief on his face fell to a stone expression of remorse, something Eloise spotted from afar. She walked past her dozens of friends, making a beeline to the grumpy old man.

"Sorry about your car," Eloise said. "I heard they drove her hard and that she needs... an overhaul? A new tranny? I don't know the lingo."

"All taken care of," Clayton said. "A local car club saw us in the news and volunteered to work on her. They raised the dough on the internet to rebuild her engine and transmission. She's fit as a fiddle again. Turns out a lot of knuckleheads love those damn crows of yours."

"I'm so glad," Eloise said. "I know how much Marilyn means to you..."

Clayton clutched her by the shoulders and looked her in the eye, something the arrogant storyteller rarely did. "It's just a car," he said. "I'm just happy you're back. We all are."

He opened the passenger door of the Cadillac and gestured for Eloise to get in.

"I just got here," Eloise said. "Where are we going?"

"Just a leisurely drive around the property," Clayton said. "I ain't taking you back to the booby hatch if that's what you're worried about."

"Let's take Virginia, too."

"I'm fine right here," Virginia said from the food table. "I have cake to serve. Just hurry back before it's all gone!"

Eloise didn't argue with them. She sat on the red leather bench seat, never imagining she'd ever get the chance. Clayton shut her door and walked around the front of the car to get behind the wheel.

"I don't recall you ever giving anyone a ride," she said.

"You're the first, sweetheart." He started the engine, but turned to look at Eloise. "Actually, you're the *second* person to take that seat."

Clayton reversed out of the horse stable and drove Eloise around Lionheart Park. He turned on the radio. Paul Anka crooned "Put Your Head on My Shoulders" as they toured the property, offering a unique view of her home she'd never seen. The majestic Victorian house surrounded by simple studio cottages felt new from the front seat of the vintage car. It felt like paradise.

"I ain't never told anyone why she's called 'Marilyn'," he said.

"I always figured it was named after Marilyn Monroe."

"Naw, that ain't it," Clayton said, laughing. "I was always more keen on Mamie Van Doren and Rita Hayworth."

"So where does the name come from?"

"Marilyn Cooper was my wife," he said, finding it hard to say the words. "I never let anyone sit here with me because I thought none of you fools was worthy to so much as spit-shine her shoes. No offense."

"So why this lovely little drive?"

"I think she'd want me to take you for a cruise," Clayton said. "I think she'd agree that a fine automobile like this is wasted without a proper passenger, and that this is the closest I'll get to having her ride with me again." He exhaled, torn about confiding his long-held inner thoughts. "So now you know."

"Bernardo Goodwin was my husband," Eloise said.

"So that's where it comes from. What a lucky man he was."

"So now you know."

"Speaking of Bernardo, let's go to the garden. That's where you met that little twerp, right?"

"I met him in the woods, but we spent most of our time in the garden," Eloise said, wishing she could see him there again, pecking at the seeds and French bread she tossed him each morning. She held out little hope, having heard nothing about him since that tragic night.

Clayton drove around the west side of the property, along the cliffs overlooking the Pacific Ocean, past the cottages and redwoods until they saw the familiar sight of the stone angel that stood in its center, raising her wings and one arm to the sky. Sitting on the eucalyptus Adirondack bench was Helene, feeding a small gathering of crows. It was Eloise's first view of them in weeks.

Clayton parked beside the entrance to the Night Garden, shut off the engine, and remained at the wheel. "She's got something to show you," he said, his grizzled expression betraying a slight smile.

Eloise stepped out of the car and walked into the garden, taking a seat beside Helene.

"Good to have you back, dear," Helene said, hugging her friend.

Eloise knew the correct response was, "It's good to be back," but those words never came out as she spotted a small statue of a crow sitting at Philomena's feet, a memorial honoring the winged keepers of the garden that all started with one little bird.

"George Rollins made it," Helene said. "I couldn't believe it. None of us knew he had an ounce of artistic talent. He sculpted it in his room. He said it was the first time he made something with his hands in twenty years."

"How is he?" Eloise asked, afraid of the many different responses she didn't want to hear.

Helene knew her friend wasn't referring to George or Clayton or any other resident. "My friends at the Audubon Society did everything they could to take very good care of him."

"How is he?" Eloise repeated.

Eloise turned and cried upon seeing Bernardo mixed in with nine other crows on the cobblestone, including Boxer, Butch, and Brandywine. The rest of the murder – a hundred other crows that bonded with the Lionheart seniors – were nowhere to be found. Perhaps they remained high in the redwoods beyond the garden, or perhaps they flew to a new roost hundreds of miles away with the thousands that joined them. She hoped it was the latter.

"They tell me he might never fly again," Helene said, unable to look Eloise in the eye. "But he's alive. He's a survivor, like you."

His wings delicately wrapped in gauze, just as they had been for so long, Bernardo dropped a piece of bread and hopped across the garden to her, looking up at her with his black marble eyes. She reached down and picked up the crippled crow, cradling him in her arms and bundling him in her macramé scarf like a newborn baby.

"I wanted him to stay with me forever," Eloise said, holding back tears. "But I also wanted to see him soar in the sky again."

"Maybe he will. One day. Only time will tell."

Eloise, Helene, and Bernardo sat and watched the crows on the cobblestone for a few more minutes before joining the rest of the awaiting residents at the party.

Lynn Harrod

THE QUEENS
ANGEL

a novel

LYNN HARROD

Abel Grant spends his days at an abandoned motel. His only friends are a prostitute who lives next door, a former gangster who protects him, and a reverend who sends him desperate folks seeking a miracle. Indeed, miracles happen at that old motel. With the touch of his hand, Abel can heal the sick, calm the troubled, and even turn back near-death. It's a gift that came to him at a terrible price, one that haunts him daily.

The Queen's Angel is a character study about what happens when an astonishing gift is bestowed upon a man who's lost his faith, and what powerful, immoral men will do to take it.

About the Author

Lynn Harrod is an award-winning writer, artist, filmmaker, and educator with over 30 years of experience crafting short stories, essays, and screenplays. His characters often find their worlds spun sideways by a startling revelation.

Lynn was awarded the PRSA Image Award of Excellence and has placed in the Quarterfinals and Semifinals of the Nicholl Fellowship, the Finals of the Nevada Film Office Competition, the Semifinals of the Writers' Network Competition, and twice in the Semifinals of the FadeIn Awards.

Born in Texas, raised in California's San Joaquin Valley, educated and trained in Hollywood, Lynn is a writer and partner with Only Human Productions, where several of his works are in development. When he's not spending time with his wife and daughter, or writing all night on his patio, he's usually having a pint with friends.

www.ingramcontent.com/pod-product-compliance
Lightning Source LLC
Chambersburg PA
CBHW060354180626
46817CB00008B/3011